SLOW WOLF AND DAN FOX

The deck was stacked against an innocent man 'til four of a kind bought into the dangerous game. The four were Larry and Stretch, Slow Wolf, the nervous half-breed, and Dan Fox, the shrewd badge-toter. Not for the first time, Larry Valentine played detective. Not for the first time, his investigation propelled the Texas Trouble-Shooters into a gun-blazing fight to the finish.

MARSHALL GROVER

SLOW WOLF AND DAN FOX

A Larry & Stretch Western

Complete and Unabridged

LINFORD
Leicester

First published in Australia in 1989 by
Horwitz Grahame Pty Limited
Australia

First Linford Edition
published 1997
by arrangement with
Horwitz Publications Pty Limited
Australia

British Library CIP Data

Grover, Marshall
    Larry & Stretch: Slow Wolf and Dan Fox.
    —Large print ed.—
    Linford western library
    1. Australian fiction—20th century
    2. Large type books
    I. Title
    823 [F]

    ISBN 0–7089–5040–X

Published by
F. A. Thorpe (Publishing) Ltd.
Anstey, Leicestershire

Set by Words & Graphics Ltd.
Anstey, Leicestershire
Printed and bound in Great Britain by
T. J. Press (Padstow) Ltd., Padstow, Cornwall

This book is printed on acid-free paper

1

The Time Element

IN Vista Ford, seat of Platt County in the Utah Territory, Blade's Cafe had closed at 8.45 this eventful night. It was exactly 10 p.m when the proprietor, Andy Blake, opened his back door to a late and unexpected visitor. He was taken aback to find himself confronted by an Indian.

"Got deer-meat to sell," the redman informed him. "Shot this morning, salted too. Fresh. Heap good."

Andy Blake, like other frontier cafeowners and hotel-keepers, had purchased game from itinerant trappers and hunters, but had done little business with Indians. Well, he could sure turn that sizeable bundle hefted on his visitor's shoulder to a tidy profit; venison steaks, venison stew would add variety to his bill of fare, and this Indian appeared harmless enough, a pudgy, swarthy character in buckskin blouse and britches, moccasins and a battered beaver hat with a turkey feather sticking up from the rear of its band.

"I'll take a look at it — and a good sniff too," he growled. "Bring it in, dump it on the table there."

As he obeyed, the redman glanced at the clock on the kitchen's inside wall. Blake, craggy-faced, five feet ten inches and stoop-shouldered, unwrapped and carefully inspected the venison. Good stuff, he decided, as fresh as the redman claimed. He made an offer. The redman grunted and nodded. Money changed hands, after which Blake watched the Indian cross the back alley, mount a dun horse and depart unhurriedly.

Blake hefted his purchase down to his cold cellar, climbed back up to the kitchen and resumed his chore, slicing bacon for tomorrow morning's breakfast customers. He was alone at this time, his wife, Irma, and daughters Grace and Jenny attending a meeting of the ladies church committee.

Also at 10 p.m. at the bakery three and a half blocks down-town, the bachelor brothers Ellis and Peter Wilton were hard at work, a side window open as relief against the heat of the ovens. It was the elder brother, Ellis, who heard the anguished yell just outside that open window and promptly nudged perspiring Peter.

Bright light from the bakery's lamps lit the area beyond the window, giving the brothers a clear view of a scene that chilled their blood. Peter loosed a shocked gasp. Hearing him, a man rose hastily from beside the prone figure sprawled face down and retreated toward the gloom of the rear of the side alley. His walk was familiar to the bakers, his clothing also.

"Holy Moses, Pete . . . !" began Ellis.

"I s-s-see it," faltered his brother.

The prone man wasn't moving; the

3

wooden handle of a knife protruded from his back.

"There'll be a deputy patrolling," mumbled Ellis. "You go find him while I take a look at — oh, hell — the poor jasper's got to be dead."

"And we know who put that knife in him," fretted Peter. "No mistake, Ellis. We both saw him clear enough — both saw Andy Blake!"

"Blake must've gone loco," Ellis said shakily. "Go on. Go fetch the law."

When the scrawny, hook-nosed Deputy Bay Thursby hustled into the alley a few minutes later with Peter Wilton at his heels, the other Wilton had set a lamp beside the body and was staring at it.

"I haven't touched anything," he assured Vista Ford's most ambitious law officer.

Thursby dropped to his knees and leaned close to study the murder victim's face. He swore triumphantly the brothers thought.

"It's Jud Daneman!" he exclaimed.

"Young Jud! Richest citizen of the county — butchered before his twentieth birthday!" He rose and grasped the elder brother's arm. "Pete says Blake did this!"

"It was Andy Blake — we'd know him anywhere," sighed Ellis. "Good man, Blake. I don't know what could've made him — do something so awful."

"He threatened Jud last week," grinned Thursby. "And look at that knife. See the B burned into the handle? Blake brands every knife he owns, his meat cleavers too. Man, oh man! Jud Daneman killed and I'm gonna go pick up the killer right now. Listen, one of you go wake the sheriff, one of you fetch a doc." Vista Ford's population had grown steadily in recent years. The county needed more than one medico, but the closest was Dr Simon Elcott. The younger brother made for the Elcott home while Ellis hurried to where Sheriff Warren Kepple lived and Thursby ran all the way to Blake's Cafe.

5

Within the quarter-hour, the cafeowner was in a cell of the county jail and indignantly protesting his innocence. Doc Elcott had made a preliminary examination of the body before ordering it removed to the Hawtrey funeral parlor. The bakers having heard the victim's death cry at exactly 10 o'clock, Elcott unhesitatingly declared that to be the time of death. And, predictably, a local busybody was riding fast to the vast Box D ranch to break the bad news to the victim's stepmother and the foreman.

Rostered to work the midnight to sun-up patrol, the other deputy entered the sheriff office at 11.35 p.m. with the intention of fixing himself a pot of coffee before relieving Thursby. Fox was his name, Daniel Francis Fox, and he was as brawny as Thursby was scrawny, a heavyset flat-nosed veteran with the beginnings of a double chin and a thickening girth. Georgia-born and carrying a badge in territory inhabited mostly by northerners, Fox would never be as ambitious as Thursby. And there were other dissimilarities. He tended to think before speaking or acting and was scornful of spite, which was one of Thursby's failings.

He paused on his way to the stove and glanced at the turn-key perched on the stool under the gunrack. The cellblock door was open, angry voices well and truly audible.

"What the hell's goin' on in there?" he demanded.

Mert Gorcey was lame and no youngster, but Fox respected him as one mighty tough and reliable jailer. Suspenders kept Gorcey's pants up, but a shellbelt was buckled in the region of his belly-button. The holstered Colt was positioned above the jailer's right buttock. No way could a prisoner make a grab for Gorcey's pistol in a desperate bid to make a break. Gorcey always faced inmates, never turned his back on them till he was well out of arm's length.

"You ain't gonna believe it," he predicted.

"Ain't gonna believe what?" prodded Fox.

"They got Andy Blake in there, holdin' him for murder," said Gorcey. "And wait till you hear who got it. Young Hot Pants Daneman. In the alley 'tween the Wilton Bakery and Govett's Hardware, one of Blake's knives in his back."

"Bull," snorted Fox. "Blake'd never . . ."

"Trouble is them Wilton brothers saw him clear," said Gorcey. "Why would they lie? They never had anything against Blake nor he against them."

Fox begged the jailer fix coffee for him and moved into the jailhouse. The cafeowner was pacing his locked cell in agitation and, not to Fox's surprise, Thursby had appointed himself interrogator. Sheriff Warren Kepple wasn't trying to get a word in edgewise. Just standing there, blinking nervously. Always nervous, Fox reflected, covertly studying his boss. Kepple was running

8

to fat, losing his hair and, in Fox's opinion, what intestinal fortitude he had ever had. Box D had always been the ruling force in Platt County, thanks to the compelling personality of Big Al Daneman who had founded it, prospered, imposed his will on the entire citizenry and finally died, a victim of his excesses, booze and gluttony, leaving his ranch and fortune not to Arlene King Daneman but to the sole issue of his first marriage, his son Judson. Fox couldn't remember a time Kepple wasn't intimidated by Box D and its unruly bunkhouse gang, a double dozen hell raising hard cases.

"You might's well confess, Blake," grinned Thursby. "The Wiltons' got a clear look at you before you snuck away and, like the damn fool you are, you left your own knife in young Jud's back," He exhibited the murder weapon. "Gonna deny it's yours?"

"It's one of mine, sure!" The prisoner came to the bars of his celldoor and glared at Thursby. "But I've been missing one for a week, damn it!"

"You tagged Jud into that alley at ten o'clock tonight, knowin' he always took that shortcut," accused Thursby.

"I was in my kitchen at ten o'clock," retorted Blake. "And, sure, I know — and a lot of others know — that alley's a short-cut to a whorehouse, the kind of place Jud Daneman visited every time he was in town — damn womanizer."

"You hated his guts," growled Thursby. "A lot of witnesses ain't about to forget you threatened him in your place, threatened to take a knife to him."

"I'm not denying threatening him," nodded Blake. "I also kicked him out and I'd do it again. The nerve of that lecherous whelp, trying to paw my Jenny, daring to touch her!" He appealed to Kepple, who promptly averted his eyes. "Sheriff, I didn't kill him. I've never killed *anybody*. That's what I told Thursby when he dragged me out of my own place with the back door left open. Damn! Irma and the girls'll be out of their minds worrying about me!"

"They've — uh — been informed," mumbled Kepple. "Your wife said something about a lawyer."

"I shouldn't *need* a lawyer," protested Blake. "How could I be in my own place and in that alley at the same time? You see my sprouting wings? The bakery's a long way downtown, more than three blocks! The Wiltons made a mistake!"

"The hell they did," sneered Thursby. "You're the one they saw and they'll swear it in court."

Fox now threw in his ten cents worth. Blake's was his favorite eating place; he knew the family and was on first name terms with the cafeowner.

"Might help, Andy, if you can recall what you were doin' ten o'clock," he suggested.

"What I'd be doing *any* night around that time," said Blake. "I fetched up a side of bacon from the cold cellar. I

11

was cutting off rashers, cutting ham too, ready for the breakfast trade."

"Buyin' in, huh?" Thursby challenged.

"Just bein' a regular lawman," said Fox. "In case Warren and you forgot, we're supposed to check *both* sides of a thing like this. A man's innocent till he's proved guilty."

"How much more proof do we need?" demanded Thursby.

"Andy, I know this was Irma and the girls' committee meetin' night," said Fox, "but were you all by yourself around that time? Was your back door open? Maybe some citizen came by and stuck his head in long enough to howdy you, somethin' like that."

"Wait a minute!" breathed Blake. He grimaced and rubbed at his temples. "Damn and blast. Thursby got me so fired up, I forgot about the Indian."

"Aw, come on!" chuckled Thursby. "Hasn't been any damn Injun seen hereabouts for all of two years!"

"There was one of 'em in town tonight," insisted Blake. "I don't know

12

if anybody else saw him, but *I* sure did. Hell, I should've remembered rightaway. I saw him and he saw me. We were in my kitchen and it was ten o'clock, same time you claim I was downtown in that alley."

"This is rich," leered Thursby. "An Injun in your kitchen."

"What was he doin' there?" asked Fox. Blake recounted the brief transaction, his purchase of a quantity of fresh venison from a pudgy redman who savvied English well enough to make himself understood. "And you're dead sure of the time?"

"I swear it was ten when he rapped on my door and I let him in," declared Blake. "And my clock keeps good time."

He scowled at Thursby. "You can have it checked if you don't believe me."

"You think I'm stupid, Blake?" jibed Thursby. "No citizen'd be fool enough to let an Injun through his doorway that time of night."

"Well, for pity's sakes, he wasn't warpainted nor aiming a tomahawk at me, you jackass!" flared Blake. "He was toting a sizeable hunk of good deermeat and it's in my cellar now."

"He hang around?" prodded Fox.

"No," said Blake. "Headed slow up the alley on a dun."

"Fat feller, huh?" frowned Fox. "Was he rigged like a white?"

"Beaver hat, but with a feather in the band," recalled Blake. "Buckskin blouse and pants. No boots. Moccasins."

"Might be a chance, if he headed north, he'll nightcamp along the riverbank," Fox remarked to the sheriff. "I'd better go look for him. Don't reckon you'll argue about that."

"Well . . . " Kepple began uncertainly.

"I believe Andy," said Fox. "And that Injun's the only one can put him in his own kitchen the time the Wiltons claim he was knifin' young Daneman."

"Circuit Judge Ewing'd never let a damn Injun testify, even if there was an Injun," warned Thursby.

"We don't know that for a fact," countered Fox. "It'll be up to the judge, right?" He didn't wait for Kepple's permission, just turned on his keel, saying over his shoulder, "If that lone Injun's still around, I'll find him."

In the office, he gulped down a cup of coffee. Then he bee-lined for the barn where his dapple stud was stabled.

The redman wasn't hard to find. North of town, in sight of the stoutly-constructed bridge spanning the Green River, he glanced away to his right and spotted the glow of a campfire. He wheeled the dapple, rode to the near bank and began following it southward.

The redman, full name Cathcart Pettigrew Slow Wolf, was in fact a half-breed, but no detail of his looks, including the color of his eyes, indicated a white woman had borne him. He looked all Sioux, though his wasn't the mentality of a warrior. He

15

felt no alarm now, as he rolled from his blanket. One rider approaching, but not stealthily, so he assumed — he fervently hoped — he had nothing to fear.

In truth, this flabby, nomadic misfit scared easily. There were times when, in a crisis situation, he accorded himself the right to self-defence, but this happened rarely. At his mother's knee — she had been a schoolteacher — he had learned English, excellent English. He *thought* in excellent English but, among palefaces, resorted to the mode of speech expected of 'dumb Injuns' with only a little knowledge of the white man's language. This, he had found, was less injurious to his health. Well, many a paleface, especially the semi-illiterates, seemed to resent — violently — a redman whose speech was in such sharp contrast to theirs.

He wasn't reaching for his Winchester when Fox rode into the firelight. The bulky deputy dismounted, ground-reined his animal, glanced at the dun, then traded stares with the seated man and said,

"How."

"How," responded Slow Wolf.

Fox came over to hunker beside him.

"Me lawman," he offered, patting his badge. "Name, Dan Fox. You got name?"

"Slow Wolf."

"Sioux, huh?" A nod from Slow Wolf. "You in town tonight?" Another nod. "All right, you tell me what you do."

"Me no steal, no break white man's law."

"Ain't sayin' you did. Just tell me where you went and what you do."

"Sell deer-meat. White-eyes give me wampum for deer-meat."

Fox's eyes gleamed.

"Know his name?"

"Blake, maybe."

"What d'you mean — maybe?"

"See that name in front. He no tell name, but maybe him Blake."

17

Coaxed by Fox, Slow Wolf recounted in his broken English the short visit to the cafeowner's kitchen. Fox then put the vital question.

"What time this happen?" Slow Wolf raised his hands and spread his fingers. "Ten o'clock?"

"Ten," said Slow Wolf.

"You speak straight? Ten o'clock for sure?"

"Speak straight. Ten o'clock."

"How you know?"

"See clock."

"You can read time by white man's clock?"

"Read time good. Short arrow point to number ten. Long arrow straight up. Number twelve."

"Clock workin', couldn't've stopped?"

"Hear good. Hear tick, tick, tick."

Until this moment, Slow Wolf was merely curious. Now, with the lawman explaining that he was an important witness, that the man Blake would stand trial for a murder committed some distance from the cafe, that he was the only living soul who could provide Blake with an alibi that could clear him, his idle curiosity gave way to alarm which he struggled to conceal. Confound the luck! He preferred to keep a low profile to avoid arousing the enmity of white men and to keep secret his superior education. Could he guard his secret in a court of law while testifying, always assuming the local authorities would accept him as a witness? What if, under cross-examination, he relaxed his vigilance and gave his secret away? Another good question; why did these things have to happen to *him*?

"You savvy?" challenged Fox.

"Savvy," he sighed.

"What it means," Fox carefully explained, "is you stay right *here* till we know if the judge'll let you make medicine in court. You savvy duty?" Slow Wolf nodded. "Fine, Slow Wolf, because that's what it gets down to. You got a duty and, by damn, if you're an honorable Injun, you'll do your duty."

"Will do duty," promised Slow Wolf.

"No go away?"

"No go away. Stay here."

Satisfied, Fox remounted and headed back to town to report Andy Blake's witness would make himself available when and if required, much to Sheriff Kepple's consternation, Deputy Thursby's chagrin and Jailer Gorcey's amusement.

Slow Wolf built up his fire, rolled into his blanket and, before closing his eyes, did some heavy fretting. His wanderlust was second nature to him; Slow Wolf Senior might as well have been a Navajo. It disquieted him to be pinned down this way, bound by a gentleman's sense of duty. Come what may, he had no option, he realized.

'You may be spared this infernal annoyance,' he consoled himself. 'It's entirely possible the presiding judge — and probably the local administration — will reject the proposition of a redskin testifying for the defence, in which case I'll be free to go my way.' But was that what he really wanted?

What of Blake's predicament? Without his testimony, that unfortunate and undoubtedly innocent man would be convicted and executed as a murderer.

Slow Wolf finally closed his eyes and slept.

But two other nomads camped some distance east were being denied slumber. Blankets draped over their shoulders, two disgruntled drifters of Texas birth squatted by their fire, chain-smoked and discussed what seemed to them a problem, but would have seemed to others a blessing.

Their names were Lawrence Valentine and Woodville Emerson, but they were better known to friendly frontier folk and unfriendly frontier lawmen and law-breakers as Larry and Stretch. Larry was the dark-haired one, the muscular hombre six feet three inches tall minus boots. Being a full three inches taller than his partner and of rangy, gangling physique, tow-haired Stretch's nickname was apt.

The problem? Their joint bankroll

stowed in Larry's wallet. They had better than $1,700 between them and, on their standards, this was just too much dinero for a couple of fiddle-foots whose needs were so humble, their needs being provisions enough, whiskey enough, tobacco enough and ammunition enough. True, they were lucky gamblers, hadn't been broke in a long time, could usually estimate their roll to be $500 or thereabouts, and even that seemed more than enough for them; greed had never been a failing of theirs.

"That damn shootin' contest at the Tragg City celebrations," complained Larry. "You had to be the best shot, had to win the five hundred dollar prize."

"And you had to put Butcher Brugel on his back for a count of ten, and him a professional prizefighter," accused Stretch. "You won five hundred too, runt, and we already had better'n seven hundred." He grimaced irritably. "The bigger a man's bankroll, the better his chances of gettin' bushwhacked for it."

"You've been sayin' that for days," grouched Larry.

"*You've* been sayin' it for days *too*," Stretch reminded him.

The wandering duo described by the frontier press as the Texas Trouble-Shooters, the Lone Star Outlaw-Fighters or a magnet for violence and upheaval, were not eccentric. They were inclined to over-simplification, true, but was their philosophy eccentric? Well, they didn't think so. The law-abiding rated an even break and protection from such two-legged predators as bandidos, rustlers and homicidal gun-toters. If county sheriffs, town or Federal marshals or the U.S. Army couldn't cope with the lawless, Messrs Valentine and Emerson could, and invariably did. And this had been their lifestyle ever since they mustered out of the Confederate cavalry after Appomattox, though they still protested they had never set out to build a reputation and preferred peace and quiet to gun-thunder and the sound of bunched fists meeting unguarded jaws.

Larry swore impatiently, fished out his watch, squinted at it and declared,

"This is plain loco, us thinkin' we're targets for robbery."

"It ain't pleasurin' me no more'n you," shrugged Stretch.

"We're thinkin' foolish," growled Larry. "Look at us. Is any sonofagun liable to guess we're packin' such a fat wad of greenbacks? What do we look like — rich hombres?"

"Folks mostly peg us for a couple driftin' cowhands," reflected Stretch.

"Because that's what we look like," Larry pointed out. "Hell, a fool all duded up and flashin' a big bankroll's just beggin' to be robbed, but do *we* ever do that?"

"Ain't our style," said Stretch.

"So what the hell're we worryin' about?" challenged Larry.

"Well," yawned Stretch. "When you put it that way . . . "

24

"So enough's enough," scowled Larry, flicking his cigarette into the fire. "Now we'll sleep and it don't matter for how long."

Stretch tossed another log on their fire and flopped. Before closing his eyes, he asked,

"What's it called again, the town west of here? Folks at the stage station at Heenan's Wells talked of it. We bought lunch there yesterday, remember?"

"Vista Ford," Larry mumbled drowsily. "Big place they said. And we wouldn't be headed for it at all, we could ride far clear of it, if we hadn't drunk all our whiskey."

"We got plenty of everything else," said half-asleep Stretch. "'Cept ammunition. And what's a man if he ain't got whiskey and plenty ammunition?"

"Thirsty," yawned Larry. "And havin' to count his shots if he rides into gun-trouble — and that ain't healthy."

★ ★ ★

25

By mid-morning of the following day, tension had taken hold of Vista Ford.

Ed Gaskell, editor of the territory's only newspaper, was preparing a special edition, though the whole county was now aware of the murder of Jud Daneman and the arrest of Andy Blake. Also being talked around was the alibi factor; there was speculation and, in some quarters, scepticism as to whether a Utah judge would accept the Indian camped by the river as a witness for the defence.

The sheriffs reaction was pretty much as Dan Fox expected — nail-biting apprehension. And Kepple's disquiet increased when handsome, grim-faced Gil Heisler, the Box D foreman, rode in to confer with undertaker Amos Hawtrey and make the funeral arrangements. He reported the murdered man's stepmother was in a state of shock. He did not report, but Kepple well realized, the entire crew of Box D had taken the news in the worst way. Feeling was running high against the hapless Blake and the swarthy nomad who had agreed to testify on his behalf.

Until the Colley family had resettled in Vista Ford a few weeks ago, there were only two resident lawyers, Sam Alper, the county attorney, and Harley Forbes, who had drawn up the will of the late Big Al Daneman and handled all Box D's legal business. It was known Forbes had refused to defend Blake and that Irma Blake had interrupted the Colleys' breakfast to beg the tyro to take the case and that young Marcus Colley had accepted a token retainer. This Fox learned when, at the end of his shift, he followed his habit of stopping by the cafe for breakfast.

Not many customers, he noted, as Jenny, the elder sister, served him.

"Bad time for you girls and your ma, but stay hopeful," he urged the girl. "Keep thinkin' of Andy's ace in the hole, the Injun. And that young Colley feller, maybe he's new to the law business, but he seems like a smart one. Family man just like Andy, purty wife and a couple kids."

"Ma's brave," frowned Jenny. "Grace and me're trying to be like her — but there's so much to fret about, isn't there? Jud Daneman was a showoff and a bully and not many townfolk liked him, but they were — and they still are — afraid to stand up to Box D. What if the foreman can't control those rowdy Box D hands? There could be a riot in town. They might — might . . . " Her bottom lip trembled, "try to — lynch Pa."

"Won't be no lynchin' — get that notion right out of your purty head," growled Fox.

"We know you'd do your best," she murmured. "But Sheriff Kepple isn't a hard enough man, is he? And we all know Deputy Thursby sides with Box D."

"I said there'll be no lynchin' in Vista Ford," scowled Fox. "And you can believe me."

She gestured worriedly.

"Just you and old Mister Prowse here for breakfast," she sighed. "Our regulars are staying away, and you know why."

"Chicken-livered," Fox said in disgust. "Don't want to be seen patronizin' the place, fearin' to show support for Andy's womanfolk. Well, you tell your ma and your sister to quit frettin', hear? Judge Ewing'll *have* to let the Injun testify. I got a real strong feelin' about that."

The Colleys were living in premises leased to them by the mayor, Efrem Stover, who owned several buildings bordering Main Street. It was suitable for a small family, the ground floor offering the young lawyer ample office space, a kitchen at the rear doing double duty as a dining room, bathroom also downstairs and, upstairs, a small parlor and two bedrooms, the larger one shared by Marcus and Linda, the smaller accommodating their sons. Young Lucas was home for lunch, the county school being located only a ten minute walk away. It would be some time before little Stevie's education began; he was still highchair age.

Over lunch, slender Linda studied her husband anxiously. He was slight of build, five feet six inches tall and scholarly-looking, a young man dedicated to his profession and determined to succeed."

"Your first murder case, Marc. Before we pooled our savings and resettled here, you'd defended only petty offenders and handled deeds of title and other humdrum matters."

"Not much hope of making my mark back in Kirsten," he reminded her. "We like Wyoming I know, but I had too much competition in Kirsten. It wasn't any bigger than this town and there were four other lawyers there. Please don't concern yourself, my dear. Win or lose, I'll give Andrew Blake the best defence possible." He grinned, but without bravado. "Vista Ford will know there's a new lawyer in town, young, but no amateur."

"The consultation?" she asked.

"On my way as soon as we finish lunch," he announced. "To the county jail to present my credentials and demand what is my right, a discussion with my client in strict privacy. The accused probably spent a restless night, but he's had time to think, perhaps to remember details. There'll be something, Linda, you'll see. A hook, an angle, a notion, something on which I can build a convincing defence."

When Marcus Colley walked downtown to the county jail, the potential witness for the defence was still camped by the river and, from the east, two trouble-prone Texans unhurriedly making their way toward Platt County along the stage trail.

Present as Marcus entered were Kepple, the tall, keen-eyed county attorney, Ray Thursby and the jailer. He voiced his request and was called a damn fool by Thursby, who warned him he'd make himself mighty unpopular by trying to defend the killer of the county's richest rancher. Marcus took exception to this, and so did Alper.

"The least a defence attorney's entitled to is courtesy," he warned the deputy. "Warren, you're the one should reprimand Thursby. I don't know why you don't."

"Well . . . " shrugged Kepple.

"I won't call you a fool, young feller," Alper assured Marcus. "I'll just express my sympathy. This'll be your first court appearance since you resettled here, right?" Marcus nodded. "Too bad your first case has to be open and shut, no hope of an acquittal. I'll do you the courtesy of summarizing the prosecution's case."

"I would appreciate that, Mister Alper," said Marcus.

At trimming the facts to the bone, Sam Alper was an expert. His short discourse covered the sighting of the murderer by reliable witnesses, identification of the weapon as Blake's own property and the threat heard by other diners the evening Blake expelled the victim from his place of business. Marcus thanked him again, after which he was conducted to his client's cell. Gorcey relocked the door and limped back to the office while Marcus perched on the bunk beside the grim-eyed Andy Blake, who got in the first word.

"My only witness is an Indian, so your most important chore will be to talk the judge into letting him testify for me."

Marcus set his derby beside him and scratched his dark thatch.

2

A Talent for Mayhem

THE prisoner was understandably edgy. He complained of his lawyer's perplexed expression, pointing out that such obvious uncertainty was no comfort to a man wrongly accused of murder.

"I do beg your pardon, Mister Blake," frowned Marcus. "It's just — there's no precedent — at least none that I know of. Possibly it's happened before. The judge may recall such a case. Of course you're absolutely right. As he's your only witness, it will be up to me to plead he be heard, and you may be sure it'll be a strong plea. This Indian, he was actually . . . ?"

"Unloading good venison on me and being paid a fair price for it," Blake nodded vehemently, "at ten o'clock, the exact time the Wilton brothers claim they saw me." He clamped a hand to Marcus's shoulder. "Listen, you're young, just getting started. If I'm gonna put my life in your hands, there's one thing I have to know right here and now and I'll thank you to look me in the eye when you answer this. Do *you* believe I put that knife in Daneman?"

Marcus's eyes didn't waver.

"If I believed you guilty, I'd not have accepted a retainer from Mrs Blake," he declared. "A decent person, a lady. And I believe you have two daughters of unchallengeable character? No, Mister Blake, I have a mental picture of you threatening the deceased and ejecting him from your restaurant, but I don't see you, a man with a good wife and two fine daughters, blighting their lives by following the deceased into an alley and stabbing him in the back." Quickly, he produced notebook and pencil. "Important point that. One of your own knives, is that right, and easily identified?"

"Right," said Blake. "Must've been stolen some time before. I was missing a knife — *that* knife."

"What kind of fool would leave his own easily identifiable knife in his victim's body?" muttered Marcus. "A good question for the jury, the seed of a doubt to be planted in their minds. Now there arises an even more vital question. Please think, Mister Blake. Is there anybody of your acquaintance to whom you bear a strong resemblance?"

"Do you suppose I haven't racked my brain trying to recall such a man?" sighed Blake. "There just isn't anybody. I have kinsmen of course, two brothers, four cousins, but they look nothing like me, they aren't killers and they live hundreds of miles from here. In fact none of them settled in Utah."

"This Indian . . . " began Marcus.

"Dan Fox already talked to him I'm told," said Blake. "He's called Slow Wolf and he savvies enough English to know what a promise means, and

36

he's promised to stay put."

"I should talk to him as soon as possible," decided Marcus. "Deputy Fox could direct me to his camp, so that'll be my next move."

Blake checked his watch as Marcus rose to leave.

"He'll have slept off his midnight to dawn patrol by now. You'll likely find him at my place."

Half-way through his lunch, Fox listened to Marcus's question, agreed he should parley with Slow Wolf and recommended a livery stable.

"Rent a horse, head for the bridge, then double back south along the riverbank. I trust that fat Sioux. He'll still be there."

Some little time later, the young lawyer was walking his hired mount along the Green's west bank, sighting the rising smoke from the redman's fire, the bridge still visible in the background.

It was a new experience for him, reining up, politely greeting an impassive

Indian and offering his name. As he dismounted, the redman responded, "Me Slow Wolf."

"Yes, Deputy Fox described you," he nodded. "It's important that we — uh — have some talk. I will speak simply to be sure you understand, Slow Wolf." He seated himself. "Because, you see, I'm in charge of Mister Blake's defence. I'm his lawyer. If the judge allows you to testify — that means talk at the trial — I will ask you to speak of how you sold deer-meat to Mister Blake at the time a man was murdered."

"Me savvy," Slow Wolf assured him.

Marcus made ready with notebook and pencil.

"In your own words, would you now repeat — say again — what you told Deputy Fox?"

With some regret, Slow Wolf mumbled it all in broken English. This young lawyer, so courteous, so patient, had made a favorable impression. He would have enjoyed discussing the case in depth, employing his above-average fluency in the language he preferred, but it was the same old story; appearances were against him. So the estimable Mr Marcus Colley must continue to treat him as a 'dumb Injun'.

Marcus took notes and was more than satisfied. The redman's testimony was proof of his client's innocence — if acceptable to the judge and jury.

"The other lawyer, he is called the prosecutor, will have the right to cross-examine," he warned. "That means . . . "

"He ask questions too," said Slow Wolf.

"And he will make angry talk," explained Marcus. "May try to frighten you, to bully you. It's his duty, you see, to discredit your words." He rephrased that. "Mister Alper will try to make you nervous, not sure, so the people will think you are not a good witness. Slow Wolf, I hope I'm making myself clear. I never had to instruct a — a man of your race — before."

"Me savvy," said Slow Wolf.

Then he winced and glanced to his left. A thud of hooves heralded the coming of riders. He counted four as they came into view, roughlooking waddies, ranch-hands, and sensed this would not be a sociable visit. He also noted the horses' brands — Box D.

As they reined up, one of them grinned contemptuously and remarked, "Well now, look what we got here, boys."

"The kid-lawyer that's sidin' Blake," observed another.

"And the stinkin' Injun that's gonna lie for him, claim Blake didn't put his knife in Jud."

"See here, this is highly irregular," Marcus protested, rising. "My client's guilt has yet to be proven. Until he stands trial, you've no right to debate the evidence with me."

"Better button your mouth, lawyer-man," growled the third man. He dismounted; his companeros followed suit, advancing threateningly. "It don't pay to stand against Box D, understand? We're mournin' a good buddy. That's what Jud was to us, buddy as well as boss. And, if you think you or the Injun're gonna talk up for Blake — that lousy killer — you got another thing comin'."

"Slow Wolf will do his duty," declared Marcus. "And I'll do mine."

"You're gonna change your mind about that," he was told.

Slow Wolf took the first blow, a savage backhander that threw him prone. In vain, Marcus raised an arm to protect himself. The assailants were big men and strong. A fist exploded in his face and, as he reeled, his head rang and he tasted blood. He fell, began struggling upright, but was winded by a boot slamming to his belly. Slow Wolf, trying to pick himself up, was felled again by a fist.

How much of this torture could he endure? This was the question bedeviling Marcus, shocking him, as

41

another man kicked him. He knew real fear now, fear he'd never felt before. These thugs were devoid of conscience, sadists, subhuman.

His cry of pain was audible to the strangers now crossing the bridge. The Texans at once drew rein and stared southward. Stretch, squinting against the sun, swore softly.

"One of them hombres takin' a lickin' — I'd bet my saddle he's . . . !"

"You wouldn't lose your saddle," growled Larry. "That's Slow Wolf for sure. C'mon — *hustle*!"

They finished the crossing, wheeled their mounts and followed the bank southward at a gallop and the urgent movements of Larry's sorrel and his partner's pinto alerted the Box D men, who whirled to study them warily. The sorrel and pinto were reined to a fast halt as Larry, his gaze switching from the prone men to their assailants, barked an order, demanding they desist.

The man who had backhanded

Slow Wolf voiced a warning to the dismounting strangers.

"Mindin' your own blame business is healthier'n buyin' into somethin' that could get your heads busted."

"Climb back on your horses and get the hell outa here," snapped the one standing over the gasping Marcus.

"Real brave hombres, runt," Stretch caustically remarked. "Four against two."

"Oh, sure," nodded Larry. "Four heroes." He cold-eyed the roughnecks and jerked a thumb. "*You* climb back on your horses, *you* vamoose — while you're able."

"Hey, ain't *he* the big talker?" leered the fourth hard case. "Just him and his stringbean sidekick — and he thinks *we're* gonna back off."

"Listen, we can take you if we have to," Stretch assured him. "We ain't lyin', ain't braggin' neither. We're just tellin' you."

"You're through tellin' us anything," came the snarled retort.

Then the four charged, hurling themselves at a couple of veteran scrappers more than ready for them. And Marcus, bloody-nosed and with one eye bruised and closing, was witness to a show of brute strength and hard hitting that shocked him to the core. Not so shocked was Slow Wolf, an old and valued friend of the trouble-shooters. He was seeing nothing he had not seen before and, though it didn't shock him, it did worry him. His warrior instincts, such as they were, were dormant most times, he being a confirmed pacifist dedicated to self-preservation. Without shame, with a certain dignity in fact, he had often described himself to Larry and Stretch as a devout coward.

The first man to reach Stretch was rib-punched before he could aim a blow, then seized bodily and hurled into the shallows. He fell hard and loosed a howl of pain louder than the splash. Larry ducked a roundhouse right, slammed a left to the belly and a right to a jaw and dunked another; the man seemed to leap from the bank to land shoulders-first and submerge.

In fury, the other two landed punches without apparent effect. The one who tried to grapple with the taller Texan had his ribs dented by an elbow, after which a mighty uppercut consigned him to the shallows. Hard Case Number 4 was learning a lesson and painfully; to stand toe to toe against Larry and try trading punches was to court heavy punishment. His ribs were aching, his nose flattened and his teeth loosened when Larry's last blow mangled his left ear and sent him pitching off the bank to hit the water face-first.

"Like I said," Stretch reminded the floundering losers, after blowing on his knuckles. "We don't lie nor brag."

"Time to go," scowled Larry. "Get your wet butts out of there and into your saddles. If we have to drag you out, you'll wish we hadn't."

Dazed and in agony, the saturated losers waded to the bank. Groans of anguish, as they struggled astride their mounts, caused Marcus's scalp to crawl. He was speechless, till the four had remounted and were moving away northward.

"You — might as well have — struck them with rocks . . . !" he exclaimed. "I've never seen such . . . !"

"Don't worry about it, little feller," shrugged Larry. "Howdy, Chief. Good to see you. In trouble again, huh?"

"You hurt bad, ol' buddy?" asked Stretch.

"Good friend Lawrence, good friend Woodville," Slow Wolf mumbled gratefully.

"Slow Wolf, you know these men?" frowned Marcus, painfully sitting up.

"He's an old buddy of ours and you heard him name us," said Larry. "How about you?"

"Marcus Colley, attorney at law," offered Marcus. "I thank you most sincerely for your timely intervention, gentlemen. Those blackguards were merciless! But for you, we'd have

46

suffered even greater injury."

"Well, Mister Marcus Colley, you look like you already did a heap of sufferin'," observed Stretch. "Anything busted?"

"My ribs ache, but it doesn't hurt to breathe," said Marcus, struggling upright. "I don't think my nose is broken and my teeth seem to have survived, but my eye . . . "

"Gettin' blue," Stretch noted. "Not purty blue like the sky, Marcus. Ugly blue."

"Squat again," ordered Larry. "You might's well get the load off till we're through talkin'." He glanced at Slow Wolf. "We gonna have to doctor you?"

"Got pain," grimaced Slow Wolf. "But not bad." He proved he was still mobile by rising, trudging to the bank, dropping to his knees and bending to immerse his head. He raised himself, spluttering. "Head clear now."

The Texans had run into Slow Wolf on many memorable occasions, knew, understood and admired him, and could take a hint. Well aware of his formidable command of English, noting he was resorting to his dumb Injun mode of speech, they got the message; the young lawyer wasn't in on his secret.

"Okay now," said Larry, hunkering and fishing out his makings. "You know what comes next, Chief. We find you and young Marcus gettin' roughed up by a bunch of plug-uglies, so naturally we get curious."

"You're gonna have to tell us what it's all about," said Stretch.

"If it don't hurt your mouth, maybe *you'd* like to do the explainin'," Larry suggested to Marcus.

"It's a somewhat complicated situation," said Marcus. "However, as you're obviously friends of Slow Wolf . . . "

"From way back," drawled Stretch.

"Saved my life many times," sighed Slow Wolf.

"He's saved ours a time or two, Marcus," offered Larry. "That's why we're friends. Now what the hell's

48

happenin' and how come them waddies beat up on you?"

The trouble-shooters smoked and listened to the young lawyer's summary of the current situation. He began with the murder of the heir to Box D and the arrest of Andy Blake, then went on to explain the significance of the time element, the fact that Slow Wolf, if allowed to testify, was Blake's only hope of cheating the gallows. And he didn't play down the problem he would have to solve, the positive identification by the Wilton brothers.

"A harrowing predicament, Mister Lawrence," he said in conclusion. "But I'm committed, so I must find a solution. The obvious assumption, of course, is that the guilty man bears so strong a resemblance to my client that the witnesses mistook him for . . . "

"How about these Wilton brothers?" interjected Larry.

"Respected local businessmen," shrugged Marcus. "They run a bakery business, and it just isn't logical they'd deliberately lie about what they saw. I understand they regret having witnessed it, because there's no bad blood between them and the accused."

"Done it again, huh Chief?" Larry good-humoredly challenged. "Got yourself in a peck o' trouble without even tryin'."

"What I call a plumb crazy accident, you tradin' with this Blake hombre same time they claim he was knifin' some feller," commented Stretch.

"A fortuitous accident for my client," declared Marcus. "As things stand, the entire defence is dependent on Slow Wolf's testimony."

"Box D sounds like a lot of outfits we've tangled with," grouched Larry. "Don't care if there's a chance the wrong man got nailed for killin' one of their own. All right, Marcus, the town's close enough. Ought to be safe for you to head back now. And you don't have to fret about any other hard cases fazin' your witness. We'll be keepin' him company." He added, as Marcus rose and moved to his horse. "Better find a doc and have him check you over before you let your wife see you."

"No sense takin' chances," said Stretch. "Might be your ribs need plasterin'."

"Thank you," said Marcus, when he was mounted. "I do appreciate that Slow Wolf is now in safe hands."

Slow Wolf traded stares with the Texans and kept an ear cocked to the receding hoofbeats. Satisfied the lawyer was well out of earshot, he sighed heavily and complained,

"I hate this — just *hate* it."

"I'll bet," grinned Stretch.

"You know I abhor exposure to the limelight," the half-breed grumbled. "Can you imagine the distress in store for me if the judge rules I should testify? Me, a modest, reticent person and a devout coward, in a crowded courtroom, in the public eye, subjected to inquisitive stares, forced to endure cross-examination by the prosecuting attorney — no doubt a blustering curmudgeon full of bombastic rhetoric. A terrifying prospect indeed. No . . . " He raised a hand, "nothing you say could comfort me. I am apprehensive, chagrined and inconsolable."

"Hey, it won't be your idea of fun," Larry said gently. "But don't try to fool yourself or us. You just know, when the chips're down, you always do what's right."

"Scruples are a curse," groaned Slow Wolf.

"Relax, Chief," soothed Stretch. "You got us now. Ain't no more hotheads gonna push you around."

"I crave coffee," said Larry.

"Me too," said Stretch. "Let's us old compadres cook up a pot and chew the fat."

Back in town, Marcus had returned the rented horse and was about to make for the home of Dr Simon Elcott when he was suddenly confronted by a grim-visaged Deputy Fox demanding to be told,

"What hit you?"

"Fists and boots," winced Marcus. "While I was conferring with Slow Wolf, four Box D riders descended on us. The beating was a warning, as if you haven't guessed, but it changed nothing. I'm not a big man, Deputy Fox, but I'm resolute. I'll do my utmost for Mister Blake."

Fox loosed an oath.

"Damn the bastards! If they try it again . . . !"

"That's not likely." Marcus's face smarted when he smiled, and still he smiled. "They suffered horrendous punishment, compared to what they inflicted on us. Two strangers happened along right when we most needed help, and what *they* did to those ruffians had to be seen to be believed. I'm sure they're on their way back to Box D now — to lick their wounds. Very fortunate for Slow Wolf and me. And it's a small world, Deputy Fox. They're old friends. Slow Wolf addressed them as Lawrence and Woodville."

53

Narrowing his eyes, Fox said softly, "Lemme hear those names again."

"Lawrence and Woodville," repeated Marcus. "Tall men, to put it, mildly. Southerners I'd say, like your good self."

"Where . . . ?"

"Camped with Slow Wolf now. We need not be concerned for his safety. They'll guard him well."

"Uh huh. Okay now, you go get cleaned up. I got to do some visitin'."

They separated, Marcus resuming his walk to the Elcott home, Fox hurrying to the livery stable where he kept his horse. Moments later, the hefty deputy was again straddling his dapple and making for the near bank of the Green. As on his first visit, the campfire guided him to his destination.

First to sight the approaching rider, Stretch jumped to a conclusion.

"Another tin star and ornery as hell, comin' to bend our ears."

"You'll have no trouble with this one," Slow Wolf assured the Texans.

"Reasonable kind of fellow. In his own gruff way, he was kind to me even courteous."

"Whatever you say," shrugged Larry. "We won't throw *him* in the river — 'less he turns mean."

Fox reined up and dismounted and, for a moment, stood arms akimbo, inspecting the redman.

"What d'you say, Slow Wolf?" he demanded. "They scare you off?"

"Hurt me, but no scare me," mumbled Slow Wolf. "Good friends help me now."

"Yeah, and I know who your good friends are." Fox traded stares with the drifters. "Valentine, Emerson, I'm a deputy sheriff of this county. Fox is my handle and, when I have to, I can be plenty foxy. I just decided you're gonna have to be my friends too, so it's okay for you to call me Dan." He frowned at the pot. "Any coffee left?"

Stretch broke out a spare tin cup and filled it as the deputy hunkered beside them.

"You're no northerner," said Larry. "But you ain't Texan."

"From Georgia," said Fox. "Close enough?"

"It'll do," grinned Larry.

"All right now." Fox gulped coffee and got down to cases. "You hot shots that've nailed more killers than a dog's got fleas, you're well and truly involved in the Daneman thing, like it or not. That don't mean you'll be in cahoots with our chicken-livered sheriff nor the other deputy, who happens to be a horse's ass, but you are sure as hell in cahoots with *me*. You got that?"

"Well, hell," protested Stretch. "We ain't even rid into Vista Ford yet."

"Just listen," ordered Fox. "For starters, I'm takin' a ride to Box D to tell Heisler, the ramrod, to keep his crew in line. Valentine, you're ridin' with me. Emerson, you'll stay here with the Injun till we get back, which'll likely be sometime after sundown."

Larry raised an eyebrow in mild enquiry.

"You sound like the kind of lawman can do his own talkin', so how come you want me along?"

"You'll savvy when we get there," said Fox. "C'mon, saddle up and let's get started."

Not for the first time, Larry was being bullied — almost — by a badge-toter. But he decided, while readying his sorrel, to play a wait and see game, specifically a wait and listen game, rather than resent proddy Dan Fox.

When they were mounted and moving north, passing the bridge, Fox guessed out loud that, so far, all Larry knew was what he had learned from the Indian and the lawyer. Larry replied this was an accurate guess, adding that he and Stretch were concerned only with the welfare of an old companero. Fox waxed curious as to why the famous trouble-shooters numbered a redskin among their best friends.

"We got to know him," Larry said offhandedly. "Our trails crossed, we mixed into a few hassles, he helped us, we helped him, and that's how it goes. We trust him, that's all."

As they pushed northwest toward Box D's vast range, Fox held forth at some length, while Larry wondered why. It seemed a fair question. On almost every other such occasion, law officers had issued stern warnings that the Lone Star drifters should disassociate themselves from whatever crisis was threatening the peace of their bailiwicks. Not so Deputy Fox, who offered a comprehensive background to the murder and the arrest of Andy Blake. Larry listened to it all, the progress and prosperity of Box D, the wide influence exerted by its founder, his second marriage to a blonde beauty many years his junior, his teenaged son inheriting the Box D fortune after his father's death, Sheriff Kepple in awe of the Daneman power, Deputy Thursby's eagerness to support the Box D faction and replace Kepple as sheriff.

When Fox paused to catch his breath, Larry urged,

"Don't stop now, you're doin' fine. Next you're gonna tell me who else had a reason to shove Blake's knife in young Daneman's back."

"Kepple and Thursby ain't sparin' a thought for others that hated the kid's guts," muttered Fox. "These're just possibilities, you understand. No way I could prove anything. Arch Nader for instance. Owns the Broken Spur Saloon and craves to get into double harness with his hired singer, good-lookin' chestnut name of Sal McLeary. The thing is Jud Daneman was makin' a big play for her and maybe she hoped he'd quit cattin' around and marry her. So Nader had no chance with her — and no reason to hope Daneman'd stay alive and healthy."

"How about some hombre with a bigger reason?" asked Larry. "Does the kid's stepmother own the whole caboodle now that he's gravebait — and has anybody been courtin' her since Big

Al cashed in? I'd call that a helluva big reason. Whoever marries her marries a bonanza."

"Smart thinkin'," approved Fox. "I can name two — maybe three. The schoolmaster, Ethan Philmore, he's a bachelor-man visits Arlene Daneman all the time. Lives with his spinster sister. Good woman, Mary Philmore. Helps out at Ella Bishop's ladies store. Howie Alderley that manages the Settlers National Bank's been sparkin' her for quite a time. He's a widower with three kids growin' fast and they sure admire Miss Mary. Wouldn't surprise me if she ends up marryin' Howie."

"Think a schoolteacher ain't liable to turn killer for a chance at a fortune?" drawled Larry. "It takes all kinds, Dan."

"Seems a nice feller, Philmore," frowned Fox. "But maybe he's a deep one."

"Who else?" demanded Larry.

"Well, another jasper tryin' to court her is Rance Staley, a sportin' man,"

60

said Fox. "He's got two axes to grind. As well as hungerin' for the widow, he had *his* reason for hatin' her stepson. Young Jud was the kind ought never get into a poker party . . . "

"Sore loser," guessed Larry.

"Right," nodded Fox. "Cussed Staley one night at the Broken Spur, called him a sharper. Now I know for a fact Staley's a pro and a pro's reputation's important to him, you know? It took him a long time to live down what the kid called him, and I'm bettin' he never forgot."

"You said maybe three," Larry reminded him.

"Ain't so sure about Gil Heisler, the ramrod," mused Fox. "He tried to keep the kid in line after Big Al died — not that anybody could tight-rein that sassy young hellion — and he acts real protective to the widow, so he *could* be Suspect Number Three."

"Dan, why're we visitin' Box D right now and why am I with you?" prodded Larry.

61

"There's just somethin' I got to prove to you," said Fox. "That's as much as I'll say till we're through there and headed back to the Injun's camp."

To reach the Box D headquarters, they had to skirt a big herd and ride a fair stretch of grazeland. It was late afternoon when Larry first glimpsed the ranch-house, and what he saw surprised him. Predictably, it was big and hacienda-style, tile-roofed and double-storeyed, but he had anticipated flagged patios, flower-beds, a small army of Mexican servants and, overall, a more imposing facade. The work corrals weren't far from the main building, nor was the long, low-roofed bunkhouse. The ranch-house porch was wide and shaded. That was where the widow was playing hostess to her gentlemen-callers.

The two horsemen were in view, but not yet in earshot. From the side of his mouth, Fox identified Arlene Daneman, her visitors and the handsome, brooding man in range clothes with a shoulder propped against a porch-post.

"Some looker, huh?" he challenged.

"Some looker," Larry agreed.

"Dark-haired dude in the fancy vest is Staley. Sandy-haired one is the schoolmaster. And the one on his feet is the ramrod." Fox added, "Leave all the palaverin' to me. You don't have to say nothin'."

"Fine by me," shrugged Larry.

They reined up a few feet from the porch to be greeted by the blonde woman and, though he stayed impassive, something stirred in Larry, a gut reaction with a chill to it. Yes, she was beautiful with her glowing hair, clear complexion and gentle dark eyes, her gown accentuating a figure envied by many a county woman. He and the deputy tipped their hats as she invited them to dismount and offered coffee. Fox responded by identifying his companion as Lawrence, after which Staley and the schoolmaster rose to be introduced.

"And Mister Gilford Heisler, the foreman," Arlene Daneman offered.

Heisler eyed Larry unwaveringly. Fox declined Arlene's offer.

"Thanks, ma'am, but this's no social visit. I'm here on law business."

"Is that so?" challenged Heisler.

"Yeah, that's so," said Fox, dismounting and gesturing toward the bunkhouse. "Call 'em out, Heisler, all four of 'em."

"What four . . . ?" began Heisler.

"You know who I mean, and the bunkhouse is where they'll be," retorted Fox. "They wouldn't be fit to tend a herd nor hang around town, the slobs you sent to beat up the Injun and scare him out of the territory, not after the lickin' they took from Lawrence and his buddy."

"Deputy Fox must mean the four who returned wet and groaning," said Arlene. "Gil, I'm in charge, now that poor Jud's been taken from us. Do as Deputy Fox asks."

The ramrod glowered at Larry,

64

turned and bellowed four names. One by one, the four who had felt the weight of Texas fists emerged from the bunkhouse and approached. They moved slowly, one with an arm in a sling, one limping, the other two walking with obvious difficulty.

"Line up in front of me," ordered Fox. "I got somethin' to say and you're gonna listen careful."

Larry flicked a glance to the bunkhouse. No other hands had appeared. Heisler stood by the porch steps. Arlene and her admirers had resumed their seats. Eyeing her covertly, Larry was again disquieted by that chilly sensation in his belly.

3

'Do it Your Way'

IN arms length of the bedraggled quartet, Fox addressed them bluntly.

"No matter who gives the order, no matter how much they offer, no Box D man better lay hands on the Injun again. He's got a name, understand? Slow Wolf he's called and it might be he'll give evidence when Blake has his day in court. That makes him a witness, and the law don't take kindly to any plug-ugly tryin' to faze a witness. From here on, it's hands off the Injun."

Having delivered the warning, he mercilessly ensured it would not be forgotten. His fists jabbed hard and two of the rogues, gut-punched, gasped and doubled over. The third man clasped his hands to his belly, anticipating similar treatment, so Fox swung a boot to his shinbone. That one howled in pain and the fourth turned to flee, but not fast enough. Fox kicked his backside with such force that he fell to hands and knees.

The schoolteacher was frowning, Heisler glaring, the woman and the gambler showing no expression at all.

"My apologies, ma'am, for teachin' these no-accounts a lesson with you lookin'," Fox said with dignity. "But it's a lesson they needed on account of they didn't just beat up the Injun. They clobbered Mister Colley too, the lawyer that'll be defendin' Andy Blake, and that makes it a whole lot more serious."

"It certainly does," she agreed.

Fox was looking at her, so missed Heisler's hostile move. Larry didn't. As the foreman's right hand moved, so did Larry's, and so swiftly as to startle all watching. His Colt was out, cocked and leveled at Heisler all in one flashing blur of movement.

"I wouldn't," he said quietly.

"That was a show-off play, damn you!" raged Heisler, his face contorted. "I wasn't about to draw on Fox!"

"You weren't?" shrugged Larry. "So — my mistake, and I sure beg your pardon."

Deftly, he uncocked and reholstered his weapon. Fox glanced at him, then at Heisler, then bade the widow and her visitors goodbye and remounted. Stirrup-to-stirrup, he and Larry rode out of the yard and started southeast across Box D range.

"Satisfied?" demanded Fox.

"Satisfied about what?" countered Larry. "On our way here, you said you got to prove somethin' to me. Prove *what*?"

"Well now, you and Stretch got your own ideas about lawmen on account of you've run into all kinds," drawled Fox. "A badge-toter like me tries talkin' turkey to you, vows you can trust him, what's it mean to you? Nothin'. It's just words. You're leery till he proves he's

68

your kind of lawman. And you know what they say. Actions speak louder'n words. Now *you* answer *my* question. You satisfied?"

"Yeah, okay," Larry assured him with a wry grin. "Sure, I'm satisfied. Dan Fox is straight. The beanpole and me can trust Dan Fox. But, listen, I'd've taken your word for it. You didn't have to bring me out here to watch you give more pain to them hard cases."

"Just as well I did fetch you along," insisted Fox. "Saves time, gets you started, gives you a notion what you'll be up against. What you've seen of Heisler's told you more'n I could say about him. You got *him* sized up and, because they just happened to be there, you've likely sized up Staley and Philmore too."

Larry eyed him sidelong.

"What *I'll* be up against?" he challenged. "Just what the hell're you talkin' about?"

"Look, I never met you and Stretch

69

before today, but I've known you for longer'n I've worn a star," Fox declared. "I know it all, believe me, the thieves and killers you've nailed, the way you operate, the way you keep beatin' the Pinkertons to badmen *they're* huntin' — and the way you play detective. Could've been a Pinkerton man yourself, right?"

"Turned down an offer," nodded Larry. "That was a long time ago. Make your point, Dan."

"The point is," confided Fox, "I'm a good enough deputy sheriff, but I'm no detective. Hell, I wouldn't know how to start lookin' for the bastard that did knife Daneman."

"You're damn well *invitin'* me to buy into this mess?"

"That's exactly what I'm sayin'. And do it your way. Maybe Thursby won't get wise to you, and it's for sure Kepple won't."

"What makes you so sure I'm that good?"

"I got confidence. You can do it."

"Any personal reason you're afeared for Blake's neck?"

"He's a friend of mine. I got respect for Irma too and the girls, but most of all it makes me sick to my gut to think of the killer — the real killer — settin' Andy up. And don't tell me that thought didn't cross *your* mind."

"Oh, sure, the chief and the kid-lawyer told me how it went." Larry's grin had no more warmth than a slab of ice. "Everything I've heard smells of a set-up. Unless Blake's feeble-minded, and you'll tell me he ain't, he wouldn't leave his own knife in a dead man's back. And somethin' else. The killer had to be a local and had to know Blake's routine. He counted on Blake bein' all by his lonesome, no alibi, that time of night, his womenfolk away at some church meetin'. How could he guess, that night at exactly that time, Slow Wolf'd come driftin' into town to do some tradin', and that he'd come a' knockin' on Blake's door? One chance in a thousand, he'd've thought."

"This's what I counted on," enthused Fox. "Already you're diggin' and figurin'."

"How about the bakers that claim it was Blake outside their window?" asked Larry. "How good can they see? Do they have to wear eye-glasses?"

"Nothin' wrong with their eyes," shrugged Fox. "And the hell of it is they're as honest as Andy himself. They'd never lie."

"Never lie on purpose," Larry corrected him. "We know it couldn't've been Blake they saw, so the killer we're after has to be Blake's dead-ringer."

"That's a long shot," grouched Fox. "I keep thinkin' about it and damned if I could name one citizen of Vista Ford you could mistake for Andy."

"So," said Larry. "Sooner or later, I'll have to parley with — what're they called again?"

"The Wilton brothers, Ellis and Pete."

"Bueno. And don't worry. I won't

treat 'em heavy. It'll be just friendly talk."

"Got any other ideas?"

"Just one," said Larry. "We do know somethin' about the killer. Maybe you ain't thought of it, but . . ."

"But you think like a detective," said Fox, "so you thought of it. And just what?"

"He had to be Baker's height," opined Larry. "Think now, Dan. You've read many a handbill on a wanted man. When it comes to a description, you read of the color of his eyes if anybody noticed, color of his hair, scars if he has any, all kinds of stuff about him, but the one detail they never forget is how tall he is, right?"

"Well, sure," agreed Fox. "So he had to be of a height with Andy, but that ain't much, is it? I'd call Andy average."

"It ain't much, but it's somethin'," said Larry. "And somethin's better'n nothin'."

It was sundown when they rejoined

Stretch and Slow Wolf by the river. No other visitors, hostile or otherwise, Stretch informed them, after which Fox accepted the invitation to take a chance on supper for four cooked by the redman from provisions supplied by the Texans.

Over this meal, Larry announced that, at Fox's urging, he was about to dig into the case against Andy Blake; the announcement surprised neither his partner nor Blake's swarthy alibi. Fox then brought up the subject of accommodation.

"You jaspers gotta have a place to stay. The hell with stayin' camped here. Too many know about it and, if Larry's gonna play detective, right in town's the place for him — the place for all three of you."

"Try checkin' Slow Wolf into a hotel, you get a big argument," warned Stretch.

"I already thought of that," nodded Fox. "It could be a problem, but we don't have to fret. I got it licked."

"So where do we bunk?" asked Larry.

"Best place for you and Stretch'd be Sanford's Hotel," said Fox. "Mort Sanford'll have a vacancy, and his place is only a half a block away from where I hang my hat. I got a room at Furth's — and Slow Wolf can share it with me."

"What's Furth gonna say about . . . ?" began Stretch.

"Gordy Furth and me go back a long way," grinned Fox. "He owes me one."

"No take white man's bed," muttered Slow Wolf. "Sleep on floor."

"Sure, well, that's no hardship for an Injun," said Fox. "Important thing is you'll be safe in my room. Won't be no hothead bother you there like they bothered you here."

"No want make trouble," grimaced Slow Wolf.

"Chief, there's only one way you could make trouble, and I know you won't do it," said Larry. "If you just vamoosed, headed for the yonder and left Andy Blake with no witness, *that'd* be trouble. For *him*. The worst kind. It's lucky for him you're an honest Injun that always does his duty."

"Me no vamoose," sighed Slow Wolf.

"Dan, how long before the trial?" prodded Stretch. "Next time the judge comes to Vista Ford, right? But when'll that be?"

"Up to the sheriff to check his almanac," said Fox. "He's done that I reckon. So, by now, young Mister Colley knows how long he's got to plan Andy's defence. A rough guess, Stretch. Three weeks at the earliest, four at most."

"So you don't have to hustle," Stretch remarked to Larry.

"If I can do anything, I'll have time enough," Larry said hopefully.

"No if," countered Fox. "You've done it before, nosed out many a killer, and you're gonna do it again."

"No promises," frowned Larry.

76

"Hell, Dan," protested Stretch. "He was born curious and he's smart-brained, but he's only human."

"I got confidence," declared Fox.

"Want to start rightaway, runt?" asked Stretch.

"Only one thing I want to check after we rent a room," said Larry. "That'll be enough for tonight. Better I hit the hay early and start fresh manana."

They were through eating. Fox drained his cup and suggested they break camp and head into town. Gear was packed and the pinto and dun saddled, the fire doused with water. With the burly deputy as their guide, they ambled their mounts west from the river to enter the county seat by a side street.

The horses were left at the livery where Fox kept his dapple. From there to Furth's Hotel, toting their packrolls, saddlebags and sheathed rifles, Slow Wolf and the drifters used their eyes, assessing the size of the town, noting the location of important landmarks, the county courthouse, telegraph office, stage depot and a saloon or two.

Reaching the smaller hotel, they parted company, Fox escorting Slow Wolf inside, the Texans moving on to the Sanford establishment.

Gordon Furth was short, a mite overweight and usually a genial character but, the moment he sighted the pudgy redman, he waxed indignant.

"Hell's sakes, Dan, you crazy — bringing an Indian in here?"

"Say howdy to Slow Wolf," offered Fox. "He's the feller did a little business with Andy Blake, when they claim Andy was. . . "

"*That* Indian?" gasped Furth.

"Relax," soothed Fox. "He don't have to sign the register. Nobody'll know he's here."

"What if some Box D gunslick learned of it?" Furth was sweating now. "Damn it, Dan, you know I try to keep trouble far from my door!"

"It might be the circuit judge'll let Slow Wolf testify for Andy," drawled

Fox. "So, he's gotta be ready and he needs a place to stay."

"Not *my* place!" retorted Furth.

Fox propped an elbow on the reception desk and reached across to finger the good luck piece dangling from the hotel-keeper's watch-chain. Furth winced and clenched his teeth.

"I'm kinda disappointed in you, Gordy," sighed Furth. "You that said, 'Dan, if I can ever do something for you . . .'"

"Cut it out, Dan," mumbled Furth.

"Know what it is?" Fox asked Slow Wolf.

The half-breed squinted.

"Bullet?"

"Yep, bullet," nodded Fox. "My friend Gordy here, he dug it out of a wall in Hanslow's Bar three years ago. Would've been three years, wouldn't it, Gordy? A crazy drunk took a shot at him, some fired-up grudge-toter. I declare the slug would've hit Gordy dead-centre but, lucky for Gordy, I happened to be there. Shoved Gordy and the slug missed him and plowed into the wall. Then I clobbered the galoot with the gun and locked him up, and Gordy dug out the slug and had a jeweler fix it to his watch-chain. Close call, huh Gordy? You were all shook up."

"You don't have to remind me," said Furth. "I've never stopped being thankful."

"So what's to argue about?" Fox asked mildly. "He'll stay in my room. You don't even need to put another bed in there. He don't mind sleepin' on the floor. The thing is, Gordy, he's gotta be where I know he's safe. Whole town don't have to know. Sure, Injuns don't relish bein' cooped, but this Injun understands why he's gotta stay put — and out of sight. All you gotta do is keep him fed. That askin' too much?"

"He savvy English?" asked Furth.

"Some," said Fox.

"Nothin' personal," Furth assured Slow Wolf. "It's just the young feller they claim Blake killed had some mighty rough friends, and if they found out I'd taken you in . . . "

"Scared, Gordy?" Fox's eyes narrowed. "You don't have to be. Any Box D waddy starts somethin', I'll take care of him — and he'll never know what hit him. Now I'm takin' Slow Wolf up to my room, okay? Our little secret friend. What nobody else don't know can't hurt 'em."

Furth shrugged helplessly while the redman followed Fox upstairs to his room. They moved in, he dumped his personal effects and glanced around. It was just a small room containing the bare necessities; he formed the opinion this hefty lawman was akin to his Texas friends in that, when it came to creature comforts, he was somewhat less than demanding.

The trouble-shooters, meanwhile, had checked into an upstairs double and unpacked. Now they stood at the open window scanning as much of Vista Ford's main stem as was visible from there.

"We find the Blake cafe, take a walk from there to the Wilton bakery, and that's all, huh?" prodded Stretch.

"The night's young," remarked Larry. "We could buy a drink at the Broken Spur so I can size up the hombre that runs it. Dan told me about him. Wouldn't take long. We can still turn in early."

As they quit the room, Stretch asked, "When am I gonna learn what happened when Dan took you to Box D?"

"Tell you all about it before we call it a day," Larry promised.

On Main Street, they questioned no passers-by; the Blake Cafe wasn't hard to find. From there, they dawdled downtown to the Wilton bakery, calculating the distance, assuring themselves it just wasn't possible; no way could the prisoner in the county jail have concluded his business with Slow Wolf, then hotfooted it down to the murder scene all in the space of a couple of minutes, three at most.

Larry studied the alley a while, noting the bright light shafting into it from the bakery's near side window.

"Mighty convenient," Stretch commented.

"You know it," agreed Larry. "The sidewinder that set Blake up had everything goin' for him."

"'Cept our old buddy," said Stretch.

"Uh huh," grunted Larry. "He thought of everything 'cept the slim chance Blake could prove he was in his own place when Daneman got it."

"If they'll let him prove it," frowned Stretch. "They had the chief in court another time, remember? But that was different. *He* was on trial."

"The hell with it," scowled Larry. "If they could try him for murder in Wyomin', he's got a right to be a witness in Utah. C'mon, let's irrigate."

The Broken Spur, one of the town's biggest saloons, was another place easy to find. When they entered, the barroom was crowded. But, thanks to their generous height, they were recognized by one of the two townmen sharing the saloonkeeper's private table. Ed Gaskell, editor of the Platt County *Post* was typical of his profession, keen-eyed and with a good memory for faces and the names that went with them. He was skinny with inquisitive brown eyes, a pointed nose and a chin to match.

"Well, look who's here," he remarked to his companion. "The troubleshooters with the big reputation, Valentine and Emerson no less."

Arch Nader, a well-built, well-groomed man with curly blond hair, allowed himself to be distracted long enough to watch the tall strangers advance to the bar. Until this moment, he had been hungrily following the movements of his hired entertainer, auburn-haired, bold-figured Sal McLeary, sauntering gracefully among his early evening customers, singing a much-loved frontier ballad, accompanying herself with a guitar. He grimaced resentfully.

"I hope they'll drink fast and leave

quietly," he muttered. "They're the kind get locked into brawls and cause a lot of damage, especially in saloons."

His other guest, local lawyer Harley Forbes, was a passably handsome, quietly spoken, soberly-attired man of an age with the newspaperman, whom he now challenged with a bland grin.

"Would you attempt to interview them, Ed? Rumor has it they aren't overly fond of the fourth estate."

"They don't like seeing their names in print," nodded Gaskell. "But they keep on making news, so what the hell else can they expect?"

While Larry paid for their drinks, double shots of whiskey, Stretch enquired of the bartender, "Don't that purty lady sing any happy songs?"

"Not since the killin' of Jud Daneman, confided the dispenser of cheer. "You're new here, but maybe you heard . . . ?"

"Yeah," nodded Larry. "We heard about it."

"Jud admired her plenty and I

wouldn't say she discouraged him," said the barkeep. "Well, give her time and she'll forget him — but it's for sure the Box D bunch won't."

"Takin' it bad, huh?" drawled Larry.

"There'll be hell to pay if Andy Blake's found not guilty," predicted the barkeep. "News travels faster'n our newspaper can print it hereabouts. I hear there's an Injun hangin' around and he could alibi Blake, but nobody's guessin' if Chet Ewing'd allow him in court. Circuit Judge Ewing, you know?"

Larry downed a mouthful and asked casually,

"You got an opinion, friend? Would a feller like Blake turn killer?"

"Hard to say," frowned the barkeep. "I like him, mind. But the thing is he sired a couple mighty good-lookin' daughters, real nice girls. And him and his wife're what I'd call protective. Young Jud now — don't tell anybody I said this — he figured himself for a ladies man, thought he could have any girl in town, includin' Grace or Jenny Blake. That made Blake good and mad. He barred Jud from his place and vowed, if he ever laid a hand on his girls, he'd put a knife in him — and maybe he got mad enough to do it."

He moved away to attend other customers. When he came their way again, Larry asked him to point out his boss. The barkeep gestured to a table by the northside wall. Larry glanced over there and, at once, Gaskell half-rose and beckoned.

Unhurriedly, the tall men carried their glasses to the owner's table. The newspaperman identified himself and offered to treat them to refills. They bluntly declined.

"Ed's told us who you are," said Nader.

"That gives you the edge on us," said Larry.

"This other gent is Mister Harley Forbes, a lawyer," said Nader. "I'm Arch Nader. I own this saloon and now I'm hoping there'll be no rough stuff while you're here."

"Won't be — 'less somebody else starts it," Larry assured him.

"If we got to fight our way out of a ruckus," promised Stretch, "we'll aim them we clobber at the batwings, try to move the fight out of here. We like to oblige if we can."

Larry nodded to Forbes and began a question.

"When Andy Blake has his day in court . . . "

"I'll be just an observer," said Forbes. "The prosecution will be handled by Sam Alper, the county attorney. I understand a recently arrived young feller, I think his name's Colley, has been retained as Blake's defence counsel."

"What I was gonna ask is how about the Injun," said Larry. "You likely heard of him. Is there some law says he can't be a witness?"

"The judge will have the last word on that question," said Forbes. "I can offer an educated guess, if you're interested. As the Indian may be the only defence witness, Judge Ewing may decide he should testify. I've always found Judge Ewing to be fair and impartial — as all judges should be."

Her song finished, the green-gowned redhead came to Nader's side, stifled a yawn and murmured a plea.

"Mind if I quit for the night, Arch? I'd like to turn in. Haven't had much sleep since — what happened to Jud."

"Get your rest, Sal," nodded Nader. "But — how long are you gonna mourn him?"

"I don't know if I'm mourning him really," she shrugged. "He was just another young buck making a play for me. It's just the shock, I guess."

"You have a lot of admirers, Sal," grinned Haskell. "You could take your pick of dozens."

"I will, if I ever decide to settle down," she replied. Before turning toward the stairs, she appraised the Texans. "You gents look old enough to have stopped growing," she remarked. "Just as well, huh? You'd be bumping your heads on the tops of doorways."

"We don't go into no small houses, Miss Sal," grinned Stretch.

Forbes checked his watch after Sal McLeary left them.

"Must be going," he said.

"And I'd best get on back to my office," decided Gaskell.

The lawyer and the *Post* editor departed. Nader remained seated. Larry nodded to him and returned to the bar with his partner.

"What're we waitin' for now?" Stretch asked, as Larry signalled the barkeep to refill their glasses.

"Waitin' for Nader to get off his butt," muttered Larry. "Want to see how tall he is before I leave."

"I asked a dumb question?" frowned Stretch.

"Nope, fair question," said Larry. "At Box D, I saw two local hombres standin', two that could get richer from this killin', and Nader's another.

Tomorrow, if they'll let us into the county jail, I'll find out how tall Blake is. Got my reasons. Tell you later."

They had finished their refills when the saloonkeeper rose and ambled to the faro layout. Larry watched him a moment, then nudged Stretch and made for the batwings.

"So?" the taller Texan demanded, while they were walking to the hotel.

"They're about the same height," said Larry. "Nader, a sportin' gent name of Rance Staley and the schoolteacher, Philmore."

Returning to the Sanford Hotel, they collected their key and climbed to their room. Larry dealt it all out while they prepared to turn in, the incident at Box D, Fox's insistence that he conduct his own investigation and all he had learned from the burly deputy during their journey back to Slow Wolf's camp.

"That's how you always start," mused Stretch. "How many others stood to win somethin' with that

91

knife, win somethin' or maybe even an old score. But — uh — suppose Andy Blake's taller'n any of 'em, or a whole lot shorter?"

"My hunch — the only hunch I got — blows up in my face," grouched Larry. "And I won't like that one little bit."

"And you'll get sore, and you're miserable company when you're sore, so I hope your hunch pays off," said Stretch.

"You and me both," said Larry.

Peeled down to the bottom half of his underwear, Stretch chose a bed and flopped. Larry moved to the other bed and squatted to remove his boots, and it was then his partner drawled a remark that started his scalp crawling.

"So this widow-lady, the dead kid's step-momma, she's some looker, huh? I mean, two hombres courtin' her and maybe the ramrod too. Purtier'n Sal Mcleary, is she?" Stretch turned, propped himself on an elbow and studied Larry curiously. "Whatsamatter?

Somethin' I said? I swear you look spooked."

Larry tugged off his boots, winced uneasily and tried to explain his reaction to the fair Arlene.

"Blonde and brown-eyed and purty, real babyface, so how come my belly turned cold when I looked at her? Damnedest thing. I don't savvy it. She was so all-fired gentle, and yet . . . "

"Maybe she's like Sal — the shock ain't left her," suggested Stretch. "She likely helped raise young Jud. Might be she treated him like she was his real mother."

"The way Dan talks of him, Jud Daneman wouldn't've cared what she or anybody else thought of him," said Larry. "He was a tearaway not yet of age and bossin' a rich spread, liked to throw his weight around, figured he could have anything he wanted, any woman he wanted. Well, maybe you're right. It ain't hit her yet. So, at the funeral, she'll likely fall apart."

"Kill the lamp and hit the feathers,

runt," urged Stretch. "Manana's another day."

In the parlor of the small home provided by the county for its resident schoolmaster, Ethan Philmore brooded, watching his sister performing a familiar chore; she was darning one of his socks. Despite spinsterhood, Mary Philmore's demeanor was sometimes maternal. Small wonder, he reflected, that Howard Alderley had grown so fond of her. She had become a little plump in recent years, but was still pleasant to look at, a woman ageing gracefully.

"You could do so much better for yourself," he said, discarding his cigar; it seemed to have lost its taste. "You don't have to go on keeping house for me nor working for Ella Bishop. Howie would marry you tomorrow."

"Certainly not tomorrow, since the Daneman funeral is set for two o'clock — and don't change the subject," she said. "We were discussing your courtship of Arlene Daneman." She raised her eyes to his. "Attractive,

94

eligible and the wealthiest woman in the county, now that her stepson is dead."

"I've told you, and I'm sure you believe me, it's Arlene I care about, not her fortune," he muttered.

"Of course I believe you," she shrugged. "You're in love — it's as simple as that — and you'd feel as you do even if she were the daughter of an impoverished family. I don't call my brother a fortune-hunter."

"Deputy Fox brought a stranger to Box D while I was visiting," he frowned.

"While you and Rance Staley, that flashy gambler, were visiting," she corrected. "What about the stranger?"

"I recognized him," he said. "Nobody who reads newspapers could fail to recognize him. He and his constant companion are hard men, gunfighters, and it's been said they trigger upheaval wherever they happen to be."

"As if Vista Ford needs more upheaval." She grimaced as she finished her work and set her sewing basket aside. "Box D employees defying the law, doing pretty much as they please so that peace-loving citizens live in fear of them, a weak-willed sheriff with two deputies jealous of each other — and you wonder why I'm reluctant to marry dear Howard?"

"He's the man for you," insisted her brother.

"And I'm the woman for him," she nodded. "But I've no intention of becoming his wife and a second mother to his children till we have a new sheriff, a man strong enough to control those Box D hell-raisers. I believe I can handle marriage, Ethan, but not in a troubled town." Abruptly, she declared, "I'll never believe Andrew Blake killed Jud Daneman."

"Hard to imagine he'd . . . " he began.

"Can *you* believe it?" she challenged.

"I guess not," he said.

"Which means they're holding the wrong man in the county jail," she said grimly, "while the real murderer stays at large, free to murder again. Very comforting thought, I don't think. And, meanwhile, those Box D roughnecks become even more unruly."

"One terrible thing about a murder." Pain showed in the schoolteacher's eyes as he uttered these words. "Any murder, whatever the motive. It solves no problems. Immediately after the crime, the murderer's apt to suffer the fear he has acted rashly and — made the greatest, most tragic mistake of his life."

Next morning, the day of the funeral, the Texans ate an indifferent breakfast in the hotel dining room.

In the kitchen behind her husband's office, Linda Colley had fed her children. Little Lucas had left for school. Now, having finished breakfast, the Colleys lingered over their coffee, she showing deep concern, he solid determination.

4

The Right Questions

"I WISH there were more I could do for your eye," Linda complained. "It's so undignified."

"Just the word." Marcus's sense of humor surfaced. He chuckled and remarked, "What will our new fellow-citizens think of young lawyer Colley? Such a gentleman, but sporting a black eye."

"Marc, it's not funny," she protested. "What happened to you yesterday is — just disgraceful. And you're not keeping anything from me, are you? The doctor did say . . . ?"

"Extensive bruises and abrasions, but no rib damage," he assured her.

"For a wonder," she winced.

"Yes, for a wonder," he agreed. "I did take quite a beating but, in one way, it did more good than harm."

"That's ridiculous," she argued. "How could you benefit from such an ordeal."

"Sweetheart, it strengthened my resolve," he declared, his eyes gleaming. "I told you I believe Blake's story and the Indian's, so I was already committed. But all that brutality, the crass injustice of it, has put fire into me, by Godfrey. It won't be a cautious, deferential defence attorney who clashes with the county prosecutor — it'll be a tough adversary. Moreover, I'll not be pleading with Judge Ewing that Slow Wolf be permitted to testify on my client's behalf. I'll *demand* it."

"Try not to antagonize the judge," she begged.

"I'll accord him all due courtesy," said Marcus. "But I'll be firm. It's going to be no holds barred, my dear. I believe in Andrew Blake, I trust Slow Wolf, Deputy Fox and those formidable Texans, and I'm determined to win!"

"How much time do you have?" she asked.

"Enough," he said. "The expected date is May fifteenth. And you will attend, I insist."

"Yes, my lord and master." She managed a smile. "I'm yours to command."

"My first murder trial," he said gently. "Other lawyers might prefer their wives stay away, seeing them as a distraction. It's different with us, my dear. You'll be my moral support. As well as being my wife, you're still my best girl, don't forget."

The trouble-shooters emerged from the hotel lighting their first cigarettes, appraised Main Street, busy already, then crossed to the east sidewalk and sauntered along to the Wilton Bakery. Ellis Wilton was behind the counter, his brother busy out back, when the tall men entered.

They greeted him affably, determined to keep this interview friendly and informal. The first point Larry impressed on the baker was that he bore him no ill will, had been told, and believed, he was a man to be trusted and had no intention of bullying answers from him.

"I don't wear a star — you already noticed, Mister Wilton. Like to help Blake any way I can and my partner and me, we're close acquainted with the Injun you've likely heard of."

"The one who claims he was with Blake when . . . ?" began Ellis.

"Yup," nodded Stretch. "*That* Injun."

"You don't have to talk to me," stressed Larry. "I got questions, but we're in your place of business and, if you'd as soon not parley with me, you got a right to order us out of here."

"Well, I have to say you're being fair about everything," Ellis conceded. "But I don't understand how I can help you. My brother and me told the law everything we know, they have our statements, so . . . "

"Ain't sayin' you or your brother

101

forgot anything," Larry assured him. "It's just there's a few things I'd like to know. So — do we talk?"

"Sure, ask away," offered Ellis.

"Okay," said Larry. "About the identification."

"Oh, it was Andy Blake we saw, no mistake," Ellis declared.

"Saw his face clear, huh?"

"Didn't see his face. He didn't turn around, just rose up and headed away from the light, made for the rear of the alley."

"Made a run for it."

"No, and I've wondered about that. No, he just walked away, that special walk of his."

"What's special about the way Blake walks?"

"Something about the way he picks 'em up and lays 'em down, kind of a plodding, stamping walk. And, of course, his clothes. Back of his brown derby got dented a long time ago. Most men now, they'd push a dent out, you know? But not Blake. He keeps on wearing it with that dent in the back."

Stretch fidgeted restlessly. Were these details of any use to his partner? Larry just listened while the baker repeated that Blake's clothing was familiar, a dead giveaway.

"Always rigs himself the same way?" he asked.

"Oh, sure," nodded Ellis. "Pete and me, we've never seen him in black pants, for instance, or any other color. Always grey. And that coat of his, there isn't another like it in the whole county."

"Tell me about the jacket," urged Larry.

"Checks," said Ellis. "Not loud, if you follow me, not big checks, but the only one of its kind. I can tell you that for a fact, because my brother got to admiring it and wanted one just like it, so he went to every store, every tailor in town. Wasn't any of 'em had that kind of material."

"Uh huh," grunted Larry. "Let me see if I got this right You and Pete

103

didn't see his face, but no mistake about his rig, the tile, and duds, the way he walks."

"Right," said Ellis. "And his size. And he's kind of stoop-shouldered. Sorry, friend, but that's how it was. I don't understand about the Indian and, like Pete and me keep reminding people, we got nothing against Andy Blake. Hell, there's never been an unkind word passed between him and us — and now we're wishing we'd stayed clear of that window. We'd be easier of mind if we hadn't seen what we saw."

"Sure," nodded Larry. "Well, thanks for talkin' to us."

After they quit the bakery, Stretch guessed,

"Already you're gettin' ideas."

"Damn right, and this you can believe," muttered Larry. "The skunk that put Blake's knife in Daneman ain't gonna be easy to flush out. To set it up like he did, he's got to be one cunnin' hombre."

104

"Well, if you say so," frowned Stretch.

"Meanin' what?" challenged Larry.

"You're the detective," shrugged Stretch. "You say this killer's smart, I ain't givin' you an argument, but maybe a killer can get *too* smart."

"Keep talkin'," urged Larry.

"Leavin' Blake's knife in the body was maybe *too* smart," insisted Stretch. "You just know young Marcus'll pick up that point and throw it at the jury."

"Bet your ass he will," agreed Larry. "All right now, next stop the county jail. If Dan ain't there, we;re gonna have to bully our way past a proddy deputy and a chicken-hearted sheriff, because the time's come for me to take a look at this Blake feller."

Luck was on their side. When they entered the law office, jailer Mert Gorcey was the only party present. Larry greeted him cordially and tried an amiable grin which was lost on a turnkey leery of strangers. He made his request, after which he and Stretch unstrapped their sidearms, slipped their holster thongs and placed the hardware on a desk along with their jack-knives. They then spread their arms and invited the turnkey to frisk them. Gorcey did that, but was still reluctant to let them into the jailhouse.

"I wanta know why," he growled, "a couple strangers care a damn about Blake."

"Amigo, we care a *big* damn about any jasper apt to swing for a killin' he didn't do," drawled Stretch.

"The Injun, Blake's alibi, he's an old compadre of ours," offered Larry. "And his word's good enough for us."

"Any time," declared Stretch.

"Yeah, I heard about the Injun," said Gorcey, sizing them up. "Heard he got jumped by Box D hands and worked over, the young lawyer-feller too. You the strangers dunked them heroes in the river?"

"That was us," said Larry. "And, if you think Box D's the only law in this territory, you won't let us take a look at your prisoner."

"The hell I won't." Gorcey's face clouded over. He moved a few paces, forcing them to notice his lameness. "Kepple and Thursby jump to Box D's whipcrack, but not Dan Fox and not me. I ain't had a shot of hard liquor these past four years. Wanta know why? Last time I got drunk, some of Big Al's hard cases beat up on me. Their idea of fun, you know? I was laid up for weeks with Doc Elcott doin' his best for me, and this is how I ended up — lame for life."

"Mean bunch," frowned Stretch.

"Trash," scowled Gorcey. Then he thought to mention, "Blake already got a visitor. I let Irma, his wife, into his cell."

"We won't butt in for more'n a few minutes," cajoled Larry. "Might visit him again but, right now, all we want is to look him over."

"You can do that from the passage," said Gorcey.

He unlocked the jailhouse door. The tall men moved in, advanced to the celldoor and doffed their Stetsons to the woman seated beside the prisoner on the bunk, holding his hand.

"Mrs Blake, ma'am, we beg your pardon," Larry said politely. "Only gonna be here a minute, then you can get back to talkin' private with your husband."

"Who . . . ?" frowned Blake.

"Take it kindly if you don't holler when you hear our names," said Larry. "We used our real given names when we checked into a hotel. Other half of them names're Valentine and Emerson. Slow Wolf, the Injun that sold you a hunk of venison, he's an old buddy of ours. We kind of like the young lawyer too, so that puts us on your side."

"You believe in my husband's innocence?" Irma asked eagerly.

"Yes, ma'am," said Stretch.

"Well," sighed Blake. "I'm grateful for that."

"It's nice you're grateful, but believin'

ain't enough," Larry pointed out "Proof is what the law needs."

"We're sure Mister Colley will do everything possible," said Irma.

"So're we," said Larry. "But, to get your man off, he's gonna need all the help he can get."

"From us," explained Stretch. "Well, mostly from my partner. He's good at snoopin', diggin' up the truth, stuff like that."

"That's all we got to say right now," shrugged Larry.

"You see, Andy?" Irma said encouragingly. "There are many people who believe you innocent — even strangers."

Larry didn't have to ask Blake to rise. The prisoner voluntarily came upright and moved across the cell to offer his hand through the bars of the door. The Texans shook hands with him, nodded respectfully to his wife and retreated along the passage to knock on the dealwood door.

The turnkey unlocked the door to admit them to the office, where they retrieved and strapped on their Colts. They thanked him and returned to the street, and the taller drifter at once asked,

"What d'you think, now that you've seen him?"

Larry had to postpone his answer. Dan Fox had hailed them from the west sidewalk and was crossing toward them. They paused. Joining them, he demanded,

"You gettin' lucky yet?"

"Gettin' a few ideas," Larry told him. "Just notions, Dan, but I'm workin' on 'em."

"Saw you come out of the office," said Fox. "Been parleyin' with Andy, have you?"

"Figured it was time I looked him over," said Larry. "We met his wife too. Nice lady. How's Slow Wolf doin'?"

"He's good at followin' orders," said Fox. "He'll stay locked in my room. Ain't complainin' neither. Funny about that. You'd think an Injun couldn't abide bein' stuck indoors, but he don't seem to mind."

"Well," said Stretch, "Slow Wolf's a special kind of Injun."

"I can believe that," frowned Dan. "He don't talk English real good but — can you beat this? — I think he can read!" The Texans masked their amusement. Of course Slow Wolf could read, and then some; at heart, he was a scholar. "Gave him the latest edition of the *Post* so he could look at the pictures. To kill time, you know? But I swear, if he ain't readin', he sure can pretend good."

Larry now thought to enquire,

"Any word on when the circuit-judge'll get here?"

"Yeah, May fourteenth," said Fox. "Most times, he comes in on the noon stage, the eastbound. So you can bet the trial'll start nine o'clock next day."

"Not real soon, runt," remarked Stretch. "Still gives you plenty time."

"Plenty," said Larry, with more

111

confidence than he really felt.

"Listen, I know you hot shots can take care of yourselves, so this is up to you," muttered Fox. "The funeral's set for two o'clock and it's for sure the whole Box D bunch'll be escortin' Arlene Daneman's surrey. Gonna be a big crowd. Ethan Philmore'll likely close the school so he can be there. Harley Forbes, lawyer that did all Box D's legal work, he'll show, Mayor Stover too, a lot of folks. After the buryin', there'll be Box D waddies in every saloon. So — uh — if you're out and about . . . "

"Don't worry, we'll stay out of sight," Larry assured him. "I got a mean feelin' we'll tangle with Box D again, but it won't be today. Meanwhile, about Big Al's will. Big secret, or would you know . . . ?"

"No secret," shrugged Fox. "Curly Miles was right there when Forbes read it in the big parlor at Box D. He's the ranch cook, only feller on the payroll I'm friendly with. Big Al left him a few hundred, he told me."

"So Jud got everything, but the widow was next in line," mused Larry.

"That's how it went," nodded Fox. "And there was — uh — what lawyer's call a provision. She could stay on for as long as she wanted."

"And, if somethin' happens to her?" prodded Larry. "She gets sick, dies . . . ?"

"Some cousin of Big Al's, Curly said," Fox recalled. "Oregon feller I think. In the lumber business."

He moved on to the law office and the Texans made their way to the shade tree in the patch of green that was Vista Ford's town square. Dominating the square was a statue of the territory's founder, one Jebediah Platt, and a fieldpiece of a type familiar to the trouble-shooters, ex-Union artillery. They squatted on a bench under the tree and rolled and lit cigarettes. Now, Larry could answer his partner's question.

"They're all of a height, around

five feet ten inches I'd reckon. Blake, the schoolteacher-feller, the gambler, and Nader and the Box D ramrod, Heisler."

"So it had to be one of 'em," nodded Stretch. "And we know Blake was missin' a knife about a week before the killin'."

"Right," said Larry. "The bastard that knifed Daneman made sure he'd be mistaken for Blake."

"But, hold on now, any hombre could get a brown derby and dent the back of it like Blake's, but how about the coat — no other like it, the baker said? Grey pants, no problem, but could the killer get into Blake's place and upstairs and steal the coat and get out again? Hell, runt, that'd take the wildest kind of luck."

"Ain't that the truth."

"So, if he didn't steal Blake's checkered jacket . . ."

"Has to be another way. It wasn't Blake's jacket."

"A coat exactly the same? Sure, but

where'd he get it?"

Larry was silent a while, smoking, thinking. Then he snapped his fingers.

"Long shot," he breathed.

"You got somethin'?" asked Stretch.

"Maybe," said Larry. "Don't know for sure yet. Got to talk to Blake's wife first. Come lunchtime, that's where we'll eat. Blake's Cafe."

They waited till noon. Entering the cafe, they liked what they saw and especially appreciated the appetizing aromas from the kitchen. What they didn't appreciate was the fall in trade; except for them, the place was empty. They made for a corner table and had no sooner hung their hats and pulled out chairs than a smiling Jenny Blake bustled out of the kitchen to attend them.

"I know who you are," she murmured, as they studied the bill of fare. "Mama told us. You're friends of the Indian and you're trying to help Pa."

"Aim to do the best we know how," Stretch said reassuringly.

115

"I'm Jenny," she offered. "And — land's sakes — you're Larry and Stretch, so now Pa has a real chance."

They settled for the fried chicken and, there being no other lunchers, the girl was happy to sit with them and gossip, but Larry wasn't irritated. On the contrary, he was interested in the local scene, eager for as much information as he could gather. She talked of her last years at the county school with her sister and their mutual admiration for Mr Philmore, that fine, patient teacher so skilled at expanding the knowledge of his students. Then she spoke of the widow of Box D and Larry's interest increased.

"She's so beautiful, that Arlene Daneman, despite all the losses she's suffered, first her husband, then her stepson — not that Grace and I would give him the time of day, you understand. Yes, I know this is the day of his funeral and Mama says it's wrong to speak ill of the dead, but we're respectable after all, and what girl

116

likes to be pawed at?"

"To win such a fine-lookin' lady, I guess Big Al Daneman was a mighty handsome gent," prodded Larry.

"He was a big man and impressive, but handsome?" She shook her head. "No. He was red-faced with an ugly nose and crooked teeth. His son took after him, but not physically. Mama says the first Mrs Daneman was very pretty and Jud favored her." With a wistful sigh, she mused, "It must've been so romantic, the way Mister Daneman courted his second wife. Of course that was a long time after his first wife died. He was on a business trip to Denver, Colorado. His first night there, he went to a theatre, and that's where he first saw her. She was in the show, the leading actress in a play."

The courtship must have become a topic for gossip in Vista Ford. Certainly, Jenny Blake knew the details by heart, and nothing she said bored Larry. The smitten Al Daneman had attended every other performance, the play's entire season, taking the leading lady, Arlene King, to supper after the show, plying her with champagne in Denver's best restaurants, champagne and gifts, till she succumbed to his ardor. She quit the company, they were married in Denver, after which Daneman brought his bride home to Box D.

Two more locals brought their appetites to the cafe; Dr Simon Elcott and undertaker Amos Hawtrey, because of the neutrality of their respective professions, probably considered themselves immune from the displeasure of Box D. Jenny hurried to wait on them and, by then, the Texans were drinking their coffee and Larry had heard enough to arouse his curiosity.

When they were ready to leave, Larry fished out his wallet and, like magic, Jenny's sister emerged from the kitchen and made for the short counter by the street entrance. While paying their tab, Larry put a question to Grace, distracting her from her preoccupation with his muscular physique.

"Somethin' I need to talk to your ma about, but I don't want to bother her when she's busy. What'd be a good time?"

"Two o'clock, best time I suppose," she frowned. "We won't be going to the funeral, but every place'll be closed, even the saloons, till it's over. I'll tell Mama and she'll be in the kitchen, so you could come to the back door."

"That'll be fine," he said.

"Uncle Dan — I mean Deputy Fox — says you want to help Pa," she said. "It's so kind of you, Mister Valentine."

"Hey, you don't have to Mister us, honey," Stretch said gently.

"All right." Her smile was a replica of Jenny's. "Uncle Stretch."

The tall men moved out, the taller one grinning self-consciously and repeating,

"Uncle Stretch."

"Suits you," shrugged Larry. "We're old enough to have sired 'em and they wouldn't call their own father Andy, would they? But we don't want 'em callin' us Mister, so . . . "

"Uncle Stretch and Uncle Larry," sighed Stretch. "Kind of cinches it, don't it? We ain't as young as we used to be."

"Nobody is," said Larry, shrugging again.

From 1.15 p.m. till around 1.50 p.m., they watched from the window of their room at Sanford's the activity on Main Street — townfolk moving toward the community chapel on the corner of Main and Fryer, stores, saloons and other establishments closing for the duration of the funeral, then the arrival of Box D, a black-suited Gil Heisler driving a handsome surrey drawn by a pair of blacks, the veiled Arlene Daneman in the rear seat, the vehicle flanked by Box D riders packing all their hardware and looking more like an invading army than mourners.

The church service began on time and, by then, the Texans were rapping on the door of the cafe. Irma Blake admitted them, invited them to sit with her and eyed Larry expectantly.

"Grace said there's something you want to ask me."

"And it could be important," Larry told her. "It's about your husband's coat, the one with the checks?"

"His only coat," she said with a faint smile. "He's not a vain man, you know, but he's so proud of that coat, wears it everywhere. Outside the cafe I mean."

"That's how the bakers identified him," he explained. "They didn't see the face of the man that killed young Daneman, but his clothes were mighty familiar. The grey pants, the derby dented in back — and that jacket."

"And the way he walked," added Stretch.

"Better you don't talk this around, ma'am, but it's plain the killer made himself look like your man," said Larry. "The coat now, he couldn't've stole it."

"He certainly could not," she declared. "When he's not wearing it, it hangs in a closet in our bedroom. To steal it, the thief would have to come into the cafe either from the street or this back door, then go up the stairs without being seen — which would be well nigh impossible — to get into the bedroom and then out again. No . . . " She shook her head emphatically, "it couldn't be done."

"I already found out your husband couldn't've bought it here," said Larry. "Can you recall where he got it?"

"Oh, that's easy to remember," she said. "He had a cousin, a feed and grain merchant at Polvadera, a town about two days' ride west. About three years ago, Nathan became ill and, knowing the girls and I could keep this place going, Andy paid him a visit. It's sad about poor Nathan. He recovered and stayed healthy until about eight months ago. A tragic accident. He was trampled by a runaway wagon team.

122

As for the coat, Andy was so happy Nathan was getting better during that visit three years ago, he decided to treat himself."

"So he bought that coat?" prodded Larry.

"Yes, right there in Polvadera," she nodded. "I don't know which store, but he said it was on display in the window and he tried it on and it was a perfect fit." He was stroking his jaw. She asked anxiously, "Is what I've told you any help?"

"Could be a big help," he said. "We'd better make this our secret, like I said, but here's how I figure it. To make himself look like your husband, the killer needed the coat. We better not forget there wasn't another like it in Vista Ford. Chances are, any time folks admired his coat, Andy told how he came by it, so . . . "

"So you think — somebody travelled to Polvadera just to buy a similar coat, because he couldn't buy it here?" she challenged.

"It could've happened that way," he insisted. "Anyway, I'll talk to Andy about it."

"Then you'll be headed for Polvadera?" asked Stretch.

"Might have to," said Larry. "I'm gettin' an idea but, as well as talkin' to Andy, I ought to try my hunch on Colley." He rose. Stretch rose with him and, as they reached for their hats, he reminded Irma, "Nobody else needs to know what I got in mind."

"I'm not a talkative person," she murmured, matching stares with him. "This is the explanation, isn't it? Jud Daneman was murdered by a man disguised as Andy."

"That's how it had to be," said Larry. "The coat was the clincher, so we can't blame the Wiltons for thinkin' they saw your man."

Until the funeral service had ended, until they assumed the widow and all the hired hands had returned to the ranch, the trouble-shooters rested in their hotel room. When Larry got up from his chair by the window, Stretch guessed,

"Now we lay your hunch on the young lawyer-feller."

"He needs it," Larry pointed out as they moved into the corridor. "And we can count on him to keep his mouth shut till he says his piece at the trial."

They found Marcus at his desk, in his shirtsleeves, consulting law books and scribbling on a notepad. He greeted them amiably and invited them to draw up chairs.

"I've been searching for precedents," he announced. Noting their blank expressions, he explained, "Other cases involving Indians. Legally, it's a rare situation, but I believe I can convince Judge Ewing and, under the circumstances, I doubt the county prosecutor will raise objections. Larry, I sense you're onto something."

"Might be the big argument you need," opined Larry. He repeated all he had learned of a distinctive item of apparel while Marcus listened intently. No immediate comment when he had told it all, so he conceded, "It's a long shot, but it's still a chance, and it's all I got."

A thoughtful nod from Marcus.

"Yes. If the murderer made his purchase farther afield, Salt Lake City for instance, your journey to Polvadera will be all for nothing. But you're right. You should try. When will you leave?"

"Early tomorrow," said Larry. "'Tween now and sundown, I can buy a few supplies, grub, booze, tobacco." He glanced at his partner. "Sometimes, we have to split up — no choice."

"I've been thinkin' that," drawled Stretch. "One of us has to stay here in case some hardnose tries to crowd Slow Wolf — or our lawyer friend here. Dan's good but, if there's a ruckus, he could need back-up."

"What I got to do at Polvadera'll get done muy pronto," Larry assured him. "I ought to be back inside four days. And somethin' else you should do. Have Dan introduce you to his buddy Furth, so Furth'll know it's okay for you to visit with the chief. Our buddy with the turkey feather might appreciate a little company."

From Marcus's office, the Texans visited a bar, a general store and a gunsmithery in that order. Larry's supplies were left in their hotel room and, while his partner flopped for a pre-supper catnap, he left the Sanford to walk to the sheriff's office. If there were short-cuts along the route to Polvadera, he should note them, and he now remembered, from his and Stretch's visit to Blake's cell, the wallmap right of the gunrack in Kepple's office.

He hoped to have only Gorcey or Dan Fox to deal with but, when he arrived, the turnkey was listening to the conversation of the sheriff, Ray Thursby and the Box D foreman.

"Our prisoner is well-guarded," Kepple was earnestly assuring Heisler.

"Take my word, he has no chance of escape."

"You'd better be damn sure about that," growled Heisler.

"Don't worry about it, Gil," grinned Thursby. "I don't reckon Blake'd have the guts to make a break anyway."

He and Heisler now shifted their attention to Larry, who had entered and was unstrapping his Colt. The deputy turned red and challenged him by name, demanding he state his business.

"Well," said Larry, placing his coiled gunbelt on a desk, adding his jackknife. "I ain't here to break your prisoner out of your calaboose nor set fire to the office nor spit on your floor, so you don't have to get your bowels boilin', Deputy." Pointedly ignoring Thursby, he appraised Kepple, now blinking uneasily. "Like to visit Blake for just a couple minutes but, first, you mind if I check your map?"

"I — uh . . . " began Kepple.

"Need to figure the fastest route to

Polvadera, okay?" Larry didn't wait for permission. He was already standing before the map, studying it. "Couple days ride straight west, looks like."

"The stage trail," mumbled Kepple. "You'll be travelling a little under a hundred miles. Polvadera's on the west bank of the Sevier."

"Much obliged," Larry acknowledged. "Howdy, Mert." He nodded to the jailer. "Like to open up? I won't be in there long."

"Larry Valentine, huh?" scowled Heisler. "Hot shot with a big reputation."

"A reputation for interferin' in law business," accused Thursby.

"What's Blake to you?" demanded Heisler.

"I'd tell you," Larry said as Gorcey unlocked the jailhouse door, "if I thought it was any of your damn business."

"Mind your mouth, Valentine," Thursby grimly chided. "Nobody talks to the foreman of Box D that way."

"Valentine just did," Gorcey mildly remarked. "Didn't you hear him?" As Larry moved in past him, he muttered to him, "I'll lock this door again so you and Blake can talk private. Just knock when you want out."

Larry ambled along the passage to pause at the prisoner's celldoor. Blake promptly rose and moved across to him.

"Still digging?" he asked eagerly. "Look, I don't mean to press you, but you're looking at a mighty worried man. For my wife's sake, I try to keep up a brave face. But I have to tell you it's not easy.

"Sure, you're in bad trouble," muttered Larry. "But you hang onto your nerve, hear? I'm diggin'. Damn right. Diggin' deep."

"Have you learned anything?"

"Well, one thing I know is the killer went to a heap of trouble to make the Wiltons think it was you they saw in that alley."

"Yes, I can understand that. Ellis

Wilton and his brother wouldn't lie about it, not deliberately."

"I don't have much time. Been talkin' to your wife, so I know you bought that checkered jacket in Polvadera. Think now, Andy. Where in Polvadera?"

Blake put his memory to work. He had a clear recollection of admiring the item on display in the window of a tailor's shop and of his great pleasure when, trying it on for size, he found it to be a perfect fit.

"So I went ahead and bought it, paid cash and wore it home."

"The tailor's name?" prodded Larry.

"Wish I could remember." Blake wrinkled his brow. "Short feller. A dude. Dark hair and one of those thin mustaches. No, damned if I can recall his name — except . . . "

"Except?" frowned Larry.

"It sounded French," said Blake. "Is that any help?"

"Could be," said Larry. He grinned encouragingly. "I'll tell you when I get back from Polvadera."

131

In the office, while pocketing his jack-knife and buckling his gunbelt, he thanked Gorcey and nodded to the sheriff, but strode out without sparing a glance for Thursby or the Box D ramrod.

5

Too Tough to Kill

LARRY'S departure, around 7.45 of the following morning, was low-key. His partner accompanied him to the livery stable. They talked quietly while he readied his sorrel and secured sheathed Winchester, packroll and saddlebags.

"'Tween chewin' the fat with Slow Wolf and Dan, keep your eyes peeled," he urged. "You know who to watch. Nader, the tinhorn, maybe the school-teacher and certainly Heisler."

Stretch promised,

"If I think any Box D hombres've caught on to where the Chief's stashed, Dan'll have an extra guest. They want to get at our ol' buddy, they have to come past me. Don't fret none, runt. I can handle 'em."

"I know you can," grinned Larry.

They were quitting the stable, he leading his horse, when a small boy confronted them, one of Ethan Philmore's pupils earning pre-schooltime dimes by selling newspapers. He was hawking the *Post's* special edition covering the Jud Daneman funeral.

"Paper, mister?"

Stretch had to bend double to pat the boy's head and tip him handsomely.

"Keep the change, sprig."

"Gee whizz!" The boy was thankful, also wistful. "I sure wish every other gent was so generous."

He hurried on and Stretch passed the paper to Larry.

"Somethin' to read while you're nightcamped."

Before stowing the newspaper in a saddlebag, Larry stared hard at the photograph on the front page, a head and shoulders shot of the blonde and beautiful Arlene Daneman. He grimaced, swung astride and nodded so-long.

"Be seein' you, beanpole."

"Ride safe," urged Stretch.

Well-rested, the sorrel took Larry a good distance west along the stage route and at steady speed. He swung off the trail and made for a copse thirty yards south at noon, there to spell, water and feed his animal, rustle up a fire and make coffee. Lunch would be a can of pork and beans, enough to hold him till he nightcamped.

He studied the newspaper picture of the widow of Box D, now its owner, while waiting for his coffee to brew. What was it about Arlene Daneman that so disturbed him? Never had he claimed a profound knowledge of the female psyche. The trouble shooters never bragged, though they did share a deep understanding of a broad cross-section of frontier types. But women? No. Many a member of the opposite sex had won their admiration, had demanded and been accorded their respect, sometimes their affection. Chivalrous at all times, tending to be protective in their own rough way, they had defended innumerable women in their long career of knight errantry, but in pigtails, teen-aged, in the full bloom of womanhood or in their advanced years, females and their foibles were a rare breed in their eyes. It would be a cold day in hell when Larry or Stretch boasted they understood women.

During that austere meal, he recalled to mind other Platt County women he had met. Sal Mcleary was what she was; nothing about her demeanor unsettled him. He was at ease with Andy Blake's loyal wife, clinging to her dignity under harrowing circumstances. And Jenny and Grace? likeable, uncomplicated, just a couple of pretty girls devoted to their parents and unhesitatingly putting their faith in him, never doubting he would uncover information vital to Marcus Colley's defence of their father.

Blake's womenfolk could not be compared to brown-eyed, blonde and beautiful Arlene in looks or character.

The hell of it was — what did he know of her character? Nothing. Yet seeing her in person had disquieted him and, studying this photograph now, he couldn't shake that disquiet. There was something different about Arlene Daneman, something beyond his ken.

He discarded the empty can, drained his cup, killed the fire and broke camp. Reaching the stage station, a lonely outpost known as Lauter's Hole, he decided to overnight there and make an early start on the morrow.

From Vista Ford to Polvadera *was* a two-day ride but, thanks to early rising and the sorrel's speed and stamina, he made his destination in the hour before dawn. A hostler came awake, rubbed sleep from his eyes and took charge of his horse at a stable in the heart of town, also directing him to an early opening diner, where he accounted for a king-sized breakfast.

In the early daylight, he walked the main stem of Polvadera, checking stores specializing in gents' apparel.

There were three, but only one name had a French look to it, Henri Colbert, Fine Tailoring, Reasonable Prices.

Around 8.50 a.m., when the dapper man approached, Larry was lounging by the locked streetdoor, browsing through the Platt County *Post*. He looked up, noted the dapper man's stature, his dark hair and pencil-line mustache and wondered how informative he would be.

"Mister Colbert?" he asked, folding the newspaper, tucking it under an arm.

"Henri Colbert at your service," smiled the tailor; he used the French pronunciation of his name. "My first customer. I don't usually find one waiting for me to open up." As he unlocked the door and gestured for the tall stranger to enter, he assumed, "A suit for some special occasion?"

"Ain't here to buy — sorry about that," said Larry, when they were inside. "What I need is information, Mister Colbert, and I need it bad. Be

138

mighty obliged if you'd let me prod your memory."

"And who would I be obliging?" Colbert enquired, positioning himself behind the counter, discarding his hat. "Must say your face is familiar, but I don't believe I've seen you in Polvadera before."

"First time here," said Larry. Play it friendly, he decided, as he propped his left elbow; this dude seemed genial anyway. He offered his hand. "Name's Valentine, called Larry."

"*That's* who you are," exclaimed the tailor, as if Larry hadn't just told him. "Remarkable, the likenesses achieved by photographers." He shook the proffered hand warmly. "Quite an occasion for me. A pleasure, Mister Valentine."

"Make it Larry."

"Delighted. Call me Henri. Oh, the hell with it. My father was French, but I was born in California and I answer to Henry. Want to prod my memory you say? Go ahead. Prod."

"Right. For starters, we go back three

years. There was a visitor here from Vista Ford, Andy Blake by name. His cousin, first name Nathan, was a feed and grain merchant, laid up with some kind of sickness."

"I remember Nathan Greeley. Everybody liked him. We were happy for him when he recovered. He'd still be with us but for a tragic accident . . . "

"Yeah, I know about that. Now, while he was here, Blake spotted a jacket in your window, all checks, admired it, came in and tried it on and bought it. You recall that?"

"It's coming back to me. Must've been the display model. Yes, now I remember. Great fit. It might've been custom-made for him though, of course, it wasn't."

"Checkered coat?"

"In the trade, we call it a hounds' tooth check. Actually, the pattern was — uh — slightly bigger, a little flashier than a regular hounds' tooth. When I bought that bolt from the wholesaler, I expected more orders than I've had."

"Next question, Henry. Since that time, have you made suits or jackets of that same cloth for other jaspers?"

The tailor did some thinking. Also, he consulted his order book, and a thick volume it was.

"Not much demand for that pattern. Let's see now. Uh huh. I fashioned a suit of it for a sporting man."

"Whole suit, huh? Coat and pants?"

"Right. My records show the name was Duffield. Confidentially, that fellow should never wear checks. Wrong build. He was about my height, a short man, but fat, really fat. Who else? Ah, yes. Mayor Tucker's boy. Young fellows of that age, he's only eleven, young Herbie, are rarely clothes-conscious, but I must say the boy cut quite a dash, wears it with pride to Sunday church meetings. It'll be a shame when he outgrows it."

"Anybody else?"

"Only one other order. A coat tailored just recently."

"How recent?"

"Less than two weeks ago."

Larry grinned eagerly.

"The hombre you made it for, what name did he use, and was he about five feet ten?"

"Well, judging from the measurements, he could be that height," nodded Colbert. "Rush job. I didn't have much work at the time, so I was able to cut, sew and finish the garment all in one day. I hope the gentleman's satisfied. I never saw him."

"Hold on," growled Larry. "How could you make a coat to fit a customer you never saw?"

"The purchaser, a lady, gave me the measurements," explained Colbert. "A gift for her husband, she said. Surprise gift. He'd be American I'd imagine. I can't imagine a Mexican gentleman of a higher class would appreciate the pattern."

"You mean *she* wasn't American?" challenged Larry.

"Mexican," said Colbert. "And I mean highborn. Nobility, you know?

Probably has pure Castilian ancestry."
He rolled his eyes. "Beautiful. Spoke
English with the most fascinating
accent."

Larry had taken a liking to Henri
Colbert but, at this moment, was feeling
mad enough to put his fist in his face.
Some payoff on his hunch. The two
day ride from Vista Ford — just
for this? In desperation, he unfolded
the newspaper and demanded Colbert
study the picture of Arlene Daneman.

"Couldn't it have been *this* woman?"

"Of course not," frowned Colbert.
"Senora de Cordoba, being Spanish,
is dark. This woman is fair-haired.
Listen, Larry, I'm sorry if this isn't the
information you hoped for, but . . . "

"You don't have to beg my pardon,
Henry," sighed Larry, retrieving the
newspaper. "No fault of yours." He
added vehemently, "Damn!"

"I've disappointed you," Colbert said
contritely.

"Not on purpose, Henry," shrugged
Larry, making for the doorway. "Thanks

for your time. Thanks for talkin' to me."

He walked some fifteen yards from the tailor shop, and then, like a physical blow, it hit him. She used to be an actress. The killer had disguised himself, so couldn't she have? For a woman of her experience, it would be no difficult chore. He whirled, dashed back to and re-entered the store, the expression in his eyes causing the tailor to flinch and recoil.

"Hey, I did say I'm sorry!"

"Henry, little buddy, you got a pencil?" demanded Larry.

"Practically everybody has," mumbled Colbert, opening a drawer. "But, the way you ask for a pencil, I half-expect you to pull your six-shooter on me."

"Take it easy," soothed Larry. "You and me, we're never gonna be enemies."

He accepted a pencil, spread the newspaper on the counter and worked with care. No artist he, so he had to ply the pencil slowly. And he had Colbert's full attention.

"Just what are you doing?"

"Show you in a minute," muttered Larry. He finished accentuating the curve of the eyebrows, then began darkening the blonde hair. "Female in the picture used to be on the stage . . . "

"I guess you don't mean a stagecoach, so you're telling me she was in the theatre, the show business, an actress."

"Now you're gettin' it," nodded Larry. "And she'd savvy about wigs, wouldn't she, and how to play a part?"

"All my mornings have been boring, compared to this one," declared Colbert.

Larry turned the picture.

"More like the de Cordoba woman?" he asked. "I don't reckon she dyed her purty hair. More likely she used a black wig."

"I'll be a son of a gun!" breathed Colbert. "Let me have that pencil!"

"I wasn't gonna steal your doggone pencil," protested Larry.

"I sketch a little," confided Colbert.

"I'm not very good at it, but I think I can manage this effect." He plied the pencil lightly. "You see, she wore a mantilla. I'll sketch it in and — by Judas . . . !"

Larry's pulse quickened.

"What d'you say, Henry?"

"You're right!" gasped Colbert. "It's *her*! Yes, I swear this is the lady who gave me the measurements, stayed in town most of the day and collected and paid for the coat!"

As he carefully retrieved the newspaper, Larry said firmly, "It's good you're willin' to swear to it, because you might have to do that. In court I mean. In Vista Ford, fifteenth of this month."

"As a witness?" frowned Colbert. "Well, I'm not backing off. That *is* Senora de Cordoba." He took hold of Larry's arm and pleaded. "Don't leave me dangling. What am I getting into? What's it all about?"

He had a right to ask, Larry conceded. And so, after swearing

146

the tailor to secrecy, he offered a terse but comprehensive account of the Vista Ford situation, the murder, the murderer identified as Andy Blake by the Wilton brothers, the alibi factor and the rough treatment suffered by Slow Wolf and the defence attorney.

"Up till now, all Blake had goin' for him was Slow Wolf," he explained. "This is a big break, Henry. If we have to, we can prove it was possible for another man to kill Daneman and make the bakers believe it was Blake they saw, because it's for sure you made a coat just like Blake's for the widow — and she's in cahoots with the real killer. You see how it adds up?"

Colbert was elated.

"I hope I *do* get a wire from Vista Ford, hope I *do* have to travel there and testify. It'll be the most exciting thing ever happened to me since my wedding night. Too bad you have to start back rightaway. If I introduced you to my Elsa, you'd know what I mean."

"Take your word for it, amigo," grinned Larry, turning to move out. "Remember now, don't say nothin' to nobody." From the doorway, he thought to add a plea. "And, for Blake's sake, take care of yourself, okay? Don't get sick, watch your step, don't let anything happen to you."

Within the quarter-hour, he was on the stage trail, eastbound now and with his mind busy, assessing the significance of this new information.

'Play-actors don't stop play-actin'. It's as natural to 'em as breakin' a horse to saddle is natural to a wrangler. She had that jacket made for a hombre she's in cahoots with, him that stuck Blake's knife in Daneman. Right from the start, that's how they planned it. To get away with murder, you need a patsy — and they chose Blake.'

The treachery of it, the absolute disregard for scruples, started his blood boiling. Small wonder the woman had made so deep an impression on him. And how well she had learned her craft

148

before marrying Big Al. It wasn't just the coat and a hat and pants similar to Blake's attire. She had even tutored the killer, teaching him to imitate his gait and to assume a stoop-shouldered look. So who could blame the Wilton brothers for — the hell with it. He would make the miles, get back to Vista Ford and feed Marcus Colley more than enough information to convince a jury Blake was the victim of a conspiracy.

It was getting toward 11.30 a.m. when he reined up to spell his mount. This section of the trail was barren, a straggle of rocks a few yards to the north, a boulder-littered rise some distance southeast. He moved some seven paces from the sorrel, tugged off his Stetson to wipe the sweatband, redonned it and was about to fish out Durham sack and matches when he heard the shot and felt the jarring impact of the bullet throwing him off-balance.

With a gasp of pain, he spun and

lurched, flopping across a flat rock, sprawling on its north side. He was in agony, fire in his left leg, fury consuming him. Hell, how he hated ambushers, the sneak-killers who sniped at their targets from safe cover, no warning, sure-thing bushwhackers.

The slug had embedded in his left thigh. He was losing blood and obsessed with his need to stay conscious. His bandana, wound and knotted above the wound, eased the bleeding slightly, but not his pain, not his fury. Clenching his teeth, yearning for his Winchester, he could only hold to the hope his attacker would quit that rocky rise southeast and advance closer to make sure of him.

'Do that, you lousy polecat!' he mentally pleaded, as he drew and cocked his Colt.

He waited for what seemed an eternity, not daring to raise his head for a quick scan of the area northeast. Instead, he relied on his acute hearing, waited till the clatter of hooves was audible. Listening intently, to the

150

hoofbeats, he estimated there was more than one bushwhacker. Two? No, three. Moments later, the voices reached him. Some argument, he guessed. The rifleman who had scored was claiming a kill — and wouldn't he wish he had? — and the other two insisting they should make sure. He stayed low until the sounds assured him they were in handgun range.

They weren't ready. The sudden appearance of his head and shoulders and gun-filled hand momentarily shocked them and that brief hesitation worked for him. He fired first at the rider hastily swinging the muzzle of his weapon his way and that one was dead before he toppled. The other two whipped out pistols and cut loose. A bullet ricocheted off the rock, whining, as he returned fire, hitting his second target dead centre; the man back-somersaulted over his mount's rump while the sorrel nickered and pranced clear. The third ambusher drew a fast bead and triggered again. He felt its hot wind fan his right ear, and then his Colt boomed again and the man howled, let go of his pistol and began slumping from his horse, his right arm blood-streaked. Hitting ground, he rolled and, left handed, groped for his fallen weapon.

'You stay alive,' Larry decided, taking aim again, 'long enough to talk to me.'

Pain wasn't affecting his shooting eye. His fourth-bullet struck the fallen pistol and sent it skittering away from its prone owner. Then Larry rose and limped into clear view, and the man saw death in his eyes.

Already, Larry had noted the brand worn by the riderless animals — Box D.

The man shuddered as Larry dropped awkwardly to prop himself on his good right knee; he stopped shuddering, froze in horror as the muzzle of Larry's recocked Colt pressed hard against his left ear.

"I'll have to head back to Polvadera to get my leg doctored," he muttered through clenched teeth. "Three things I can do about you — bushwacker. Leave you like this so you'll bleed to death, blow your no-good head off, or take you with me so maybe a Polvadera doc can save your arm."

"Gimme a break!" the man begged.

"Up to you," Larry said harshly. "You and your buddies weren't lookin' to pay me off for the lickin' my partner and me gave four Box D bastards. You — were followin' orders. Whose orders?" He pressed harder. "You got till I count to three. Your choice, hero. One . . . "

"Heisler — the ramrod — for a hundred apiece," came the babbled answer. "But I can't tell you why. He didn't say why!"

It was late afternoon when Larry saw Polvadera again. In agony, weak from loss of blood, he straddled his sorrel and somehow managed to maintain his hold of the reins of the other animals, two of them with dead men hung across them, the third toting

153

the wounded man, who could lose consciousness any moment.

With locals gawking at him, Larry kept going until, through a red haze of pain, he saw the shingle of the sheriff's office and a scrawny, bewhiskered badge-toter poised on the steps. As he drew rein, he called a plea.

"Don't wire Vista Ford! They — ambushed me! Don't — do nothin' — till we've talked . . . !"

He had time, just enough, to voice those words before his strength failed him. Loss of blood took its toll and the oblivion claimed him; he wasn't even conscious of falling from his mount.

★ ★ ★

Arlene Daneman traveled into Vista Ford this day at 2 p.m. seated in back of the Box D surrey with a hired hand driving. Trading talk with Dan Fox on a corner at this time, being assured by the beefy deputy that Andy Blake's witness was eating regularly and voicing no complaint against his forced confinement, Stretch gave himself an eyeful of the woman descending from the surrey in front of the Settlers National Bank. Fox identified her and parted company with him.

Rolling a cigarette, the taller Texan reflected,

'All right, runt, you said I should keep checkin' on the Chief and the lawyer-boy and keep my eyes peeled too. Widow-woman spooked you somehow, which means you're plenty curious about her. So, okay, I got to be curious as you.'

He lit his cigarette, crossed the street and lounged against a lamp-post. The facade of the bank was in full view. When she was through in there, he would give himself another eyeful.

She emerged about fifteen minutes later, spoke to the Box D man on the surrey's driving seat, but did not reboard the vehicle. The hired hand nodded and touched his hatbrim; she unfurled a parasol and moved along the west sidewalk. On the east sidewalk, Stretch began dawdling, keeping her in sight. He noticed several passers-by traded greetings with her, some pausing to talk. Just townfolk, he decided.

He was directly opposite and still watching when she reached the street doorway of an office; the inscription on the front doorway read: 'H. T. Forbes, Attorney At Law.' The door was open. She entered to be at once embraced by a man the watcher only glimpsed, but recognised. After that embrace, the lawyer hastily closed the door, and a keenly interested Stretch guessed the door would also be locked and was not surprised when the window-shade was lowered.

'Well now,' he mused. 'Here's a fine howdy-do and the same to you.'

Under other circumstances, this part of Main Street not as busy, he would have been tempted to eavesdrop. No chance anyway, he assured himself. The widow and the family lawyer craved privacy; Mr Harley Forbes wasn't fool enough to leave a side window partly open.

What would Larry make of what he had seen? He speculated while ambling to Furth's Hotel. The proprietor, now accustomed to his coming and going, offered a preoccupied nod as he entered and moved to the stairs. A few moments later he was rapping on the door of the room rented by Deputy Fox and being admitted by a swarthy friend, who carefully re-secured the door.

"How's everything, Chief?" he asked, squatting on the edge of Fox's bed.

From Fox's chair, Slow Wolf replied, "No change, no belligerent admirers of the late Judson Daneman attempting to force entry and inflict further bodily harm. And you, Woodville my friend?"

"Been hangin' around like Larry told me," frowned Stretch. "Just saw somethin' and — uh — I don't reckon I was meant to see it and neither was nobody else."

He recounted his brief surveillance on the widow of Box D and the scene he had glimpsed. The pudgy half-breed heaved a sigh.

"Ah, what a tangled web some palefaces weave," he remarked.

"Howzat again?" blinked Stretch.

"Complications, intrigue, side issues of possible significance," mumbled Slow Wolf. "The case becomes more involved, my friend. Who is to be trusted? Who lies, and who adheres to the truth? But it is not my prerogative to speculate. Lawrence would read something into it, for he has the questing mind of an investigator. The clandestine intimacy you witnessed may enlighten him, may in some measure support his theories."

"I got *some* of that," said Stretch.

"Actually, the estimable Mister Colley will be even more interested than I am," Slow Wolf assured him. "To him falls the onerous duty of preparing a convincing defence for the hapless Andrew Blake. You should convey this intelligence to him at once."

"Yup, I'll do that," nodded Stretch.

158

"But we got time on our side, Chief. Trial won't start till the fifteenth and, meanwhile, I got a hunch Larry'll score in Polvadera. He'll learn somethin' else Marcus can use, bet your ass on that."

"Indeed, yes," agreed Slow Wolf. "Remarkable, the way Lawrence's questing nose leads him to the truth."

"How're you gettin' along with Dan?" asked Stretch.

"A good soul, a credit to his race," said Slow Wolf. "Rough, stout-hearted, a man of good intentions and, of course, loyal to his friend Blake." He waxed wistful. "Loyalty — such an admirable quality."

"Andy's womenfolk, we took to 'em right off," Stretch remarked. "Regular ladies, plumb friendly. But that Arlene, she had my ol' buddy spooked first time he laid eyes on her."

"Lawrence is intuitive," declared Slow Wolf. They traded stares a long moment, then he gestured to the door. "I am safe here, my tall friend. Think of the young lawyer, laboring over his notes, rehearsing his address to the jury, searching his mind for counters to the — I don't doubt — impressive technique of his more experienced opponent, the county prosecutor. Go to him now. Report what you observed. It will be important to him."

"Sure," said Stretch, heaving himself upright. "I'll go talk to him, and you take it easy, okay? Be seein' you, Chief."

Slow Wolf saw him out and relocked the door. Descending to the street, Stretch strolled to the office and home of Vista Ford's youngest lawyer and, en route, sighted the Box D surrey departing. Mrs Arlene Daneman had concluded her business with Harley Forbes, whatever that business might be.

He entered Marcus's office to find Linda setting a cup of coffee on her husband's paper-littered desk. Marcus performed introductions. Stretch doffed his Stetson and accorded her a bow, but declined her offer of coffee, explaining he had something to tell Marcus.

"I'll leave you to it."

She smiled amiably and retreated to her kitchen. Stretch drew up a chair while Marcus sipped coffee and eyed him hopefully.

"Anything new, Stretch?"

"Somethin' I just happened to see," nodded Stretch. "Could be important. You'll have to decide." He described again the manner of Arlene Daneman's arrival at the office of attorney Harley Forbes, while Marcus's eyebrows shot up, adding, "Might be they're just old friends. I mean, he's the family lawyer after all."

"Yes, but . . . " Marcus gulped more coffee. "It could mean more. You said he was quick to shut the door and lower the window-shade. Whatever their real relationship, it's not public knowledge. That seems quite clear."

"I could go ask him where *he* was."

Stretch made this suggestion half-heartedly. "Ten o'clock that night?"

"You don't really want to do that," observed Marcus.

"My partner'd do it better," said Stretch.

"I don't think Mister Forbes should be questioned — yet," said Marcus. "But I wonder if the others have been asked to account for their movements on that fateful night, at that specific time. I'm remembering those Larry regards as alternate suspects, the saloon-keeper Nader and the gambler Staley. Again, not a chore for you. Why not ask Deputy Fox? He'd know."

"I'll go find him," offered Stretch.

He did and, listening to the suggestion, Fox grimaced impatiently.

"I'm damn sure Warren or Thursby'd never think of it and I wish I had," he growled. "Leave it to me. I'll brace 'em rightaway."

Convincing alibis, Fox soon learned. Poker party at the Broken Spur the night of the murder, the players

Nader, Staley, Mayor Stover and two local merchants of good repute. The game began around 8 p.m. and was interrupted some little time after 10 when news of the murder and Blake's arrest began circulating. The saloonkeeper who so resented the murder victims attentions to the woman he craved and the gambler with a heavy grudge had unchallengeable alibis.

Nader said, as he and Staley breasted the bar with Fox,

"You had to ask. I guess you have to cover every angle. No hard feelings and the drinks're on the house."

"I'm not mad either," decided Staley. "No denying Arch and me had our own good reasons for hating Daneman's guts."

"He'd have just used Sal," scowled Nader.

"Fifteen years I've been a sporting man — fifteen years," Staley said bitterly. "I've done it all, made bluff plays, even drawn to an inside straight, but never yet marked a deck nor dealt one from under. I play square and, for my money, a cardsharp is scum. Yet that loud-mouthed brat had the nerve, the gall, to . . . !"

"All over now, Rance," soothed Nader, as the barkeep did his duty. "He can't finish what he started, can't break Sal's heart nor challenge your honesty again."

Fox took a pull at his drink and muttered,

"Daneman can't harm nobody, but Platt County could hang Andy Blake and make misery for three good women — Irma, Grace and Jenny." He eyed the gambler sidelong. "Staley, would you hitch up with the widow, if she'd have you?"

"This very day," Staley said fervently.

6

Crisis Day, The 15th of May

WHEN Larry next opened his
eyes, his mind was fuzzy his
vision blurred, his mouth and
throat dry.

'Take your time,' he urged himself.
'Get it all together, but slow and
easy.'

He kept his eyes open. Gradually,
his mind and vision cleared; he could
move his head on the pillow, look
around, recognize familiar items. What
was he wearing? A nightshirt, and
certainly not his size. The bed was
comfortable, but this wasn't his kind of
bedroom. Big understatement. Fancy
drapes at the window, a distinctly
feminine type dressing table by the
wall to his left. The familiar items
were on a chair in a corner, his folded

underwear and other garments, all but his pants, and obviously they'd been laundered. Resting atop the pile was his coiled shellbelt and, dangling from the upturned butt of his Colt, his Stetson.

No severe pain at his left thigh, just a smarting. He drew the bedcovers aside long enough for an inspection of the wound. It was bandaged, the bandage snow-white. So he had received medical attention, the slug was out. Turning to his right, he noted the items on the bedside table, his wallet, watch, small change, tobacco and matches, a glass and a carafe. He realized how weak he was, had to, when he half-filled the glass and drank the water; his movements were labored. All right, no big surprise. He *had* lost blood. But now he was rid of the dryness of mouth and throat and could make himself heard, and did.

He heard footsteps, then the door was opening and a plump, no longer young, but brisk-moving woman came in. Her hair was hennaed. She put him in mind of a saloon-woman well past her prime and wouldn't have cared if she were ugly as sin. The smile was what mattered to him, cheery, amiable, full of reassurance.

"Ma'am . . . ?" he began.

"Great voice," she enthused, moving to his side. "Deep, hundred percent masculine, just what I expected. How're you feeling. Any nausea?" He shook his head. "Fine, so you feel kind of empty? Don't fret about that. I got beef stew simmering and Rod says it's okay for you to eat. Not only okay. Absolutely necessary, to get your strength back. Rod's my husband, Doctor Rodney Tobias, out on a call right now. Your turn now."

"Mrs Tobias . . . "

"Call me Patsy. Everybody does."

"I'm Valentine, first name Lawrence."

"My daughter's name! Some coincidence, huh?"

"You and the doc named your girl *Lawrence*?" Patsy Tobias chuckled heartily and slapped her knee; she was perched on the edge of the mattress now.

"No. Jessica. The handsome young feller she married is Joe Lawrence, owns a store in Salt Lake City. Our son Lester grew up and got married too. He and our daughter-in-law and grandchildren moved to Selmer City, Nevada. This used to be Jess's bedroom."

"How long've I been here?" he asked urgently.

"Two and a half days," she replied.

"*That* long?" he frowned. "All I got was a slug in my leg."

"Rod had to keep you sedated," she explained. "You got excited, delirious too. Listen now, we'll get some nourishment into you between now and when Rod gets back from his rounds, and then he'll decide if Sheriff Upfield can question you." She rose, flashing that cheery smile again. "Start you off with a bowl of beef broth with corn-bread in it. You get that down, you'll be ready for some meat. Be nice

168

and, when I fetch your coffee, there'll be a stiff shot of brandy in it. Red said that'd do no harm." On her way to the door, she paused for his next question. "No, George Upfield told Rod to tell you, soon as you came to your senses, he did what you begged him just before you passed out."

Larry heaved a sigh of relief. He had another question, important, but was obliged to postpone it till he'd accounted for most of the bowl of broth. What day was this? Her answer disquieted him.

"May tenth — you sure?"

"Why wouldn't I be sure?" she teased. "Ever hear of an almanac? Finish your broth and I'll bring the stew and, while you eat, I'll satisfy your curiosity about me."

"Ain't for me to be curious, Patsy," he shrugged.

"But you're curious just the same," she good-humoredly accused. "How come the likes of me got to marry a regular gentleman doctor and bear and raise two kids for him? Tell you all about it presently."

She took away the empty bowl. He began forking up cubes of stewed beef, the best he'd tasted in a long time and, to his amusement, she offered her explanation as though reciting a fairy story to a small child.

"Once upon a time, long ago, a young doc fresh out of medical school sashayed into a West Colorado saloon for a beer and the bartender was me. My brother owned the saloon and I was helping out. I was younger and, if I say so myself, quite a looker. As for Rod, he had all his hair then and was some smooth-talker. Love at first sight. We got married a month later, came here to Polvadera to start this practice and lived happy ever after. He's bald as an egg now and I'm . . . "

"Still a looker," he grinned.

"I just knew we'd get along, you and me," she smiled. "No, I'm not as pretty as I used to be, but Rod still loves me and vice versa."

"I had a newspaper . . ." he began.

"You still have," she said. "It's under your underwear. I washed your clothes, everything except the pants. The bullet tore your levis before it bored in, and I haven't gotten around to . . ."

"Don't worry about it," he said. "I got plenty cash. Next time you're in a store . . ."

"Sure," she nodded. "I know your size." With a wink, she added. "I helped undress you."

After that meal, washed down by two cups of brandy-spiked coffee, he tried to fool himself he was ready to quit the bed, but Patsy's husband put paid to that idea. He returned right after she carried the used dishes away, drew a chair up to the bed and used his stethoscope, a lean, alert-eyed healer whose surviving hair clung to his temples like ash-grey cottonwool.

"Name of Valentine, my wife tells me," he said. "All right, I hope you're a patient man — and intelligent — because it's my duty as your physician to warn you against any notion of saddling up and riding till you're in better shape — *much* better shape — than you are right now. Your recovery period has only just begun."

"I got to get back to Vista Ford by the fifteenth," insisted Larry.

"Impossible," declared Tobias. "That's only five days from now, and it'll be four more before I'll let you try your feet. After that, you'll need three days of recuperation."

"I can't stay away that long!" gasped Larry.

"Am I talking to a deaf man?" Tobias wondered irritably. "Listen, I'm not blind. I've duly noted your scars — all of them. This isn't your first gunshot wound, but it happens to be more serious than some of the others you've suffered. Now stay calm and take heed."

"You're the doctor," grimaced Larry.

"I wouldn't expect you to have any recollection of your condition when you arrived," said Tobias. "Critical

172

is the word. I estimate you escaped gangrene by a matter of mere hours and, at that, it was just freak luck. To extract the bullet, I had to probe extensively. There is irreparable tissue damage, but you're a man of powerful physique so, in time you may — I stress *may* — cease to limp. Another point. Blood loss was greater than you seem to realize. You were also feverish. Well, I did quite a job on you and I know you'll recover, but only if you give yourself *time*. Too much movement — too soon — and that wound could open. And that, my friend, could be messy — and disastrous. We're talking about a serious wound that has sapped your strength, not a shallow graze."

"I heal fast," said Larry. "I'm a big eater and Patsy — she invited me to call her Patsy — is onehelluva cook. Is it okay by you if we parley again about how soon I can move, say a couple days from now?"

"Meaning another consultation — after another examination," frowned Tobias.

"Very well, but no promises. And now, as you're in good voice, I'll advise our sheriff he can come visit you."

Less than twenty minutes later, the bearded Sheriff George Upfield was filling the chair vacated by the doctor and getting in the first word.

"I know who you are. We get the Vista Ford paper here, so I know what's happening there. My deputies and I have said nothing to anybody. The two stiffs were buried here, Doc saved the third feller's arm and he's locked tight in my jail. Your horse is resting easy in our best livery stable. The stableowner's taking care of your saddle and gear. All right, I've obliged you, Valentine. If the people at Box D are wondering what became of three of their hands, they'll have to keep on wondering as far as I'm concerned. And now — *you* talk to *me*."

Larry reached for his makings. It pleased him that he could build and light a cigarette unaided.

"Ain't gonna hold out on you," he

muttered. "You got a right to some answers and you'll get 'em, but it'll be just 'tween us, okay?'

"Why all the damn secrecy?" demanded Upfield.

"I'll tell it all," offered Larry. "Then you'll savvy the spot I'm in. You said you get the Vista Ford paper, so you already know there's gonna be a trial pretty soon."

"Feller name of Blake, for the murder of the Box D boss," nodded Upfield.

"I can help prove Blake didn't do it," Larry declared. Then he took it from the beginning, explaining his, Stretch's and Slow Wolf's involvement, describing the current scene in Vista Ford and confiding his reason for visiting a Polvadera tailor and the outcome. "So now it's a safe guess why three Box D guns tried to earn a hundred apiece for makin' sure I'd be too dead to tell what I learned from Colbert. The ramrod got wind I was headed for here, and he wants Blake to hang — not the real killer."

"Damn and blast," breathed Upfield.

"It's all up to me," fretted Larry. "Somehow, I got to show for the trial, but Doc Tobias . . ."

"Knows his business," earned Upfield. "Whatever he says about the shape you're in, you'd better believe it. And here's something you should think about. You've been stuck here two and a half days. You know Heisler set those bushwhackers on you, but you don't know if it was his idea or if he was following orders. And, by now, he'll be wondering why they aren't back yet."

"Aw, hell," grouched Larry. "He ain't just wonderin'. He'll be spooked."

Upfield lit a cigar, got to his feet and began pacing. "I know your style — troubleshooter," he growled from behind a cloud of smoke. "You're a rule-buster from way back. Well, just this once, maybe I'll play as cunning as you."

"What've you got in mind?" Larry asked warily.

"I got his name, the one I'm holding," said Upfield. "It's Bonner."

"So?" prodded Larry.

"So I'll send Heisler a wire — signed Bonner," decided Upfield. "It'll read 'Laid up in Polvadera, but job finished.' Something like that. Just enough to make Heisler believe he's rid of you. My best offer, Valentine."

Larry flashed him a grateful grin.

"And you call *me* a rule-buster."

"I'll take care of it rightaway," said Upfield, turning to leave. Then, about to open the door, he frowned back at Larry. "Hey, somebody else you forgot about."

"My partner," sighed Larry.

"He'll come looking for you," said Upfield.

"No, he'll stay put," muttered Larry. "He always does like I tell him, and I told him to help Dan Fox protect Slow Wolf and young Colley."

"Because they've already been attacked and it could happen again — that's what you think?" challenged Upfield.

"It could happen," said Larry. "So Stretch won't budge."

"He'll be fretting and you'll be running out of patience — bad combination," opined Upfield. "Well, this time, you *have* to stay patient. Doc Tobias knows what's best for you.

He went his way, leaving Larry to seethe in frustration, wondering how he could endure the waiting.

That evening, after disposing of the supper served him by Patsy Tobias, double helpings of everything and she marvelling at his Gargantuan appetite, another local was allowed visit him.

His dramatic return to Polvadera had been observed by Henri Colbert, who had bided his time, staying clear of the Tobias home until being informed by Sheriff Upfield that the casualty was now convalescing and able to converse.

"I have their permission to look in on you," he assured Larry, seating himself by the bed. "The good doctor, his genial wife *and* the sheriff. Now,

178

friend, and I hope we *are* friends, I'm here to make an offer, depending on whether or not you feel inclined to satisfy my curiosity about something."

"If you got a question, Henry, go right ahead," invited Larry.

"The way you came back to town, well, I didn't have to be a genius to guess what happened," said the tailor. "You fought your way out of an ambush."

"You got that right," nodded Larry.

"Can you tell me — is there a connection?" frowned Colbert. "What you learned from me, and then the attempt on your life?"

"Has to be," said Larry. "I told you how important your information was, and I recall I warned you . . ."

"That I might receive a telegram summoning me to testify," finished Colbert. "They'd delay the proceedings while I made the journey to Vista Ford." His frown deepened. "So it's obvious, isn't it? The ambushers didn't move fast enough to intercept you east of Polvadera, so they lay in wait for you when you were headed back."

"That's how it adds up," said Larry.

"All right, I've come to a decision," Colbert told him. "If you recover in time to return to Vista Ford for the trial, you won't have to repeat everything I remembered about the woman disguised as a highborn Mexican. I'll testify in person. When you leave here, I'll leave with you. My store will be closed a few days, but that's no great inconvenience compared with the plight of Mister Blake."

"You got a point, Henry," mused Larry. "You sure got a point."

"The right thing to do," shrugged Colbert. "A duty really."

"I appreciate it," Larry said warmly. "What's more important is Andy Blake and his womenfolk'll appreciate it."

"A duty and a pleasure," insisted Colbert. "So you'll let me know when you're ready to leave?"

"Count on it," said Larry.

For the troubleshooters, the next two

days seemed to pass at snail's pace, Larry striving to be an easy-to-handle patient in the home of Polvadera's doctor, Stretch conferring frequently with Slow Wolf, Dan Fox and Marcus Colley, all the time fretting; his old sidekick had been gone too long. Larry cursed his need to maintain secrecy; to wire Stretch was too great a risk. With the trial date drawing closer, Box D men loitering in Vista Ford could pick up the news that one Texan had been contacted by the other. And he didn't want Heisler alerted. Better Heisler should be reassured by a telegram apparently sent by George Upfield's prisoner.

On the afternoon of the thirteenth, while Tobias was redressing his wound, Larry made his pitch.

"I'm healin' good, you got to admit."

"Better than I anticipated," the medico conceded. "But . . . "

"Hear me out," begged Larry. "In Vista Ford, day after tomorrow, a man'll stand trial for murder. I learned somethin' here in Polvadera that'll help clear him, so I got to testify. It's his neck I'm talkin' about."

"Damn," scowled Tobias. "It would *have* to be a matter of life and death, so now you add to my already heavy responsibilities, my professional duty to a patient unfit to travel, the danger of an innocent man being convicted."

"And he *is* innocent," stressed Larry. "So you got to let me go. If I leave rightaway, I can make it a slow and easy ride, no hustlin'."

"Too dangerous," Tobias said flatly. "Valentine, I wish I could permit it but, in conscience, I can't. For you, a horseback journey is out of the question. If you did reach your destination, you could be suffering a relapse, losing blood, and then what? You'd be too ill to attend the trial."

"Has to be a way around this," muttered Larry. He racked his brain for a solution while Tobias secured a fresh bandage. The idea that came to him seemed the perfect answer; he put it eagerly. "How about an eastbound stage that'd get me there on the day of the trial?"

Tobias winced and shook his head.

"Easier than travelling by horseback, but not easy enough, still too much jolting. Yes, I know the trail between here and Vista Ford is fairly smooth going, but stagecoaches adhere to a timetable, have to maintain speed. The rocking motion, you trying to brace yourself — no — it just wouldn't do."

Larry wasn't letting up.

"If my horse has to stay stabled here, okay. You say I daren't ride nor hop a stage, okay. But listen now. I got plenty cash. I can afford to rent a rig and team here, I mean a *good* rig, light, well-sprung, smooth-rollin'."

"You aren't fit to drive, confound it!"

"I won't *have* to drive. There's a mighty reliable hombre gonna be travellin' with me, and he'll do all the drivin'. Look, I'll rent a double-seater if you want, and lie — not sit — on the back seat. And the earlier we get started, the easier the travellin'. He won't have to drive the team fast. We can loaf all the way to Vista Ford and still get there in time. Now how about *that*?"

It was a tough decision for Tobias, as evidenced by his troubled expression.

"Who would your companion be?"

"The tailor, Colbert. You likely know him."

"Know him well. A much-respected citizen."

"So I ask you, is he the kind of jackass that'd grab the reins and drive like crazy?"

"No, not Henry Colbert," Tobias fretted a while, then insisted, "I'll provide a cane — which you *must use*. It's vital that you favor that leg."

"Whatever you say," nodded Larry. "Now can you get word to Henry I want to see him?"

"You're determined to leave — almost immediately?" winced Tobias.

184

"Sooner we get goin', easier the travellin'," Larry reminded him. "And remember what I said about my bankroll when you make out my bill, Doc. You and Patsy, all your trouble, her feedin' and tendin' me . . . "

"All right," shrugged Tobias. "All right."

The tailor was delighted, declaring it an honor to drive a famous trouble-shooter to Vista Ford and present his testimony. Moreover, he knew the ideal rig for their purpose and a comfortable journey was assured. Larry gave him cash enough for the rental charge and, with help from Tobias, donned his laundered underwear, his new Levis and his other garments, then strapped on his Colt and proved he could move with the aid of the cane. Tobias continued to instruct him right up to his boarding the sprung two-seater with a pair of well-chosen blacks harnessed. Patsy kissed him goodbye and made him promise to visit when he returned to Polvadera for his horse.

And then, in the hour before sundown, he and Colbert were eastbound, destination Vista Ford.

★ ★ ★

As expected, Circuit Judge Chester Ewing arrived in Vista Ford mid-afternoon of the 14th and, soon afterward, Marcus Colley was summoned by Deputy Thursby to the office of the county attorney.

Ewing, a snub-nosed veteran whose spade beard was considerably less shaggy than the brows above his steel-grey eyes, was seated in Alper's desk chair. Also present when Thursby ushered Marcus in was the sheriff and the bespectacled Brice Jeffries, a justice of the peace who did double duty as court orderly.

Marcus was invited to sit. The judge, studying him in a not unkindly way, explained he had been given a general picture of the situation and asked was the defence ready. Marcus assured him he'd be ready at the court's convenience.

"Nine sharp tomorrow morning," said Ewing. "But now, young feller, I'm advised this will be your first murder trial and that, to date, your defence of Andrew Blake will be the testimony of an Indian."

"Will that present difficulties, Your Honor?" Marcus politely enquired. "It is unusual, I know, but . . . "

"I'll have to establish his capability and his full appreciation of his responsibility," Ewing pointed out. "Here and now, for instance, you may assure me he has a sufficient grasp of English, but I have to find out for myself — no reflection on your integrity of course."

"I do understand, sir," nodded Marcus.

"However, I must also adhere to procedure," said Ewing. "A jury will be selected — quickly I hope — and then, before Mister Alper's opening address, I'll have to put a few questions to — I believe Slow Wolf is the name — to satisfy myself he has full understanding of his duty."

"I believe he will satisfy you," said Marcus.

"Well, young man, you've gotten to know him," frowned Alper. "I haven't even seen him, since you decided to keep his whereabouts a secret."

"A necessary precaution against attempts to intimidate him, Mister Alper," insisted Marcus.

"Come on now . . . " began Thursby.

"Excuse me, Deputy," said Marcus. "I believe you, Sheriff Kepple and possibly Mister Alper are aware there has already been just such an ugly incident."

"Is this something I should know about?" demanded Ewing.

"Just high-spirited Box D hands venting their feelings, Judge," offered Kepple. "We have to make allowances. After all, the murder victim was Jud Daneman, their boss."

"While Slow Wolf was camped by

the river, while I was having my first discussion with him, we were set upon by four Daneman hands," said Marcus. "I being of slight physique and Slow Wolf being somewhat of a pacifist, we could do little to defend ourselves. We both took a beating, Your Honor."

"One of *those* situations," grouched Ewing. "Feeling running high against the defendant. Sheriff Kepple, I'll tolerate no disruption by unruly elements in my court. Kindly bear that in mind tomorrow. I suppose it's inevitable the courthouse will be crowded. But, at the first hint of rowdiness . . . "

"We'll — uh — keep everybody in line, my deputies and me," Kepple nervously promised.

"One thing more, Mister Colley," said Ewing. "There are limits to the concessions I can make to untried defence attorneys. I'll help where I can, but I'd better warn you you'll be up against an experienced veteran . . . " He gestured to Alper, "who has demoralized many an opponent."

"I'll try to go easy on you, sonny," smiled Alper.

"Very well," said Ewing. "If that's all, I'd like a hot bath and a nap before my supper."

From 8.30 the following morning until 9 o'clock, the area fronting the county courthouse was busy. Deputy Fox personally escorted Slow Wolf past gaping locals and into the building, Stretch according the same service to the defence lawyer and his wife. Fox then positioned himself at the entrance to ensure various parties such as the defendant's wife and daughters and the prosecution witnesses could enter and find seats before the record crowd of onlookers. The ramrod of Box D arrived with four Box D hands, lawyer Harley Forbes following, then Arch Nader and Rance Staley. Fox half-expected Ethan Philmore would show up, till he remembered this was a regular schoolday. Conspicuous by her absence, or so it seemed to Fox, was Arlene Daneman.

After Kepple and Thursby arrived with the defendant, Fox stood aside and the rush began. By 9 o'clock, when Judge Ewing took his place behind the bench, the courtroom was full and all windows open, many standees lining the side aisles.

It took only a quarter-hour for a jury to be selected, after which, the twelve good men and true being seated, Ewing requested the only non-white present to rise. Slow Wolf did so, eyeing him attentively, his feather-bedecked headgear held to his chest. The judge addressed him firmly, but patiently. How much of the white man's language did he understand, and did he realize that, having taken the oath, he would be duty-bound to speak only the truth? Slow Wolf cleared his throat and nodded respectfully.

"Savvy English good," he declared. "Tell lie after swear on good book — big sin — heap big sin. Me speak straight."

"Do you understand that, after

you have answered questions asked by the lawyer you know, you will be questioned by a lawyer you do not know?" asked Ewing. Slow Wolf nodded. "That will be Mister Alper and it will be his duty to — uh — make big argument of all you have said to the court. This you also under — savvy?"

"Savvy," nodded Slow Wolf. "Still tell truth, speak straight."

"How well do you understand white man?" prodded Ewing. "Do you have paleface friends?"

"Good paleface friends," Slow Wolf assured him. "Savvy ways of whites."

The judge studied him a moment longer, nodded for him to resume his seat and informed both attorneys, "I'm satisfied this witness is qualified to testify. You may proceed, Mister Alper."

In his opening address, the prosecutor refrained from raising his voice, but made sure every damning word was heard. He laid emphasis on the bad blood between the accused and the deceased, the threat voiced by the accused in hearing of several witnesses and the unchallengeable veracity of the brothers who identified the killer.

His first witnesses, present during the disturbance at the cafe at the time of the threat, testified as to the nature of that threat. Marcus waived cross-examination of the first two, but put a question to the third, a bright-eyed, elderly man.

"We've heard nothing from the other witnesses as to the reason for Mister Blake's anger. Can you enlighten us, sir?"

"Certainly can," said the witness. "Young Daneman was taking liberties with one of the Blake girls . . . "

"Explain that, please."

"Well, he had his hands on her and she didn't take kindly to that. Regular little ladies, the Blake sisters. That's when Blake came in from the kitchen and bounced Daneman."

"One expects better from even a tyro lawyer, Your Honor," Alper rose to protest. "The old and unpardonable tactic of sullying the character of the murder victim . . . "

"Your Honor, surely my client's motive for ejecting the deceased has some relevancy," frowned Marcus. "Was it his custom to threaten other males patronizing his place of business?"

"Objection over-ruled," decided Ewing.

"I have no more questions of this witness," said Marcus.

He waited until Ellis Wilton was repeating almost word for word the testimony of his brother before again cross-examining. Having prodded the witness into stressing the killer's familiar garb, his stature and distinctive gait, Alper smiled triumphantly.

"Your witness, my learned *young* colleague," he offered.

'Nice try, Mister Alper,' Marcus was thinking as he approached the stand. 'But goad all you want — I'll not amuse you by a show of temper.'

He nodded genially to Ellis Wilton.

"You've been most precise, sir, and I'm confident you'll be as precise in your answers to my questions. By his movements and his clothing — so familiar to Vista Ford folk — you have identified the accused as the man you saw rising from beside the body of the murder victim. But the face — you didn't see the man's face — not even a quick glimpse?"

"Not his face, no, we never saw his face," said the baker.

"Therefore, the man could have been disguised as Andrew Blake, is that not so?" demanded Marcus. "Wearing similar clothing, imitating Andrew Blake's way of walking?"

"I strongly object!" growled Alper. "Preposterous, Your Honor! The defence . . . " He had to raise his voice above jeering laughter aimed at Marcus, "invites the witness to speculate, calls for a conclusion on his part!"

"Your Honor . . . " pleaded Marcus.

"Very well, Counsellor," sighed Ewing,

as the laughter subsided. "I'll hear your counter before ruling on Mister Alper's objection."

"The proposition I put to this witness warrants not speculation but a simple yes or no reply," declared Marcus. "I guarantee to show relevancy — to the court's complete satisfaction — in my address to the jury. It is already obvious, Your Honor, that no man can be in two places at the one time. I don't mean that as levity, I assure you, but the testimony of a witness who can place the accused three and a half blocks away does I believe justify a claim of impersonation, the murderer going to considerable pains to masquerade as the accused — which is not impossible."

"Quite a submission, Mister Colley," frowned Ewing.

"Tantamount to an address to the jury," complained Alper.

"I'll sustain your objection, Mister Alper," said Ewing. "I will not, however, instruct the jury to disregard defence counsel's statement,"

"No more questions," said Marcus.

He did not challenge Deputy Thursby's identification of the murder weapon. The point would be challenged, but for the jury's consideration.

There being no more prosecution witnesses, he was directed by the judge to deliver his opening address to a jury whose interest he had well and truly aroused. He confronted the jurors, his demeanor dignified and confident despite the question plaguing him. When, if ever, would Larry reappear?

7

No Ordinary Indian

WELL to the fore in the body of the court, Linda Colley watched her husband and crossed her fingers, watched him hook his thumbs in the arm-holes of his vest and, as he began his address, hung on his every word.

"Gentlemen of the jury, the weight of evidence against my client *seems* damning indeed. I say seems damning because, and this may have occurred to many of you, it is remarkably circumstantial. Let us consider, for instance, the Andrew Blake so well-known to the people of this community, such a familiar personality, his fondness for a certain garment, his check-patterned coat, the only one of its kind ever seen in Vista Ford. Let us give some thought to the character of the man and his standard of intelligence." Moving closer, Marcus made a fist and pounded the rail of the jury enclosure. "Is my client a complete idiot? I don't believe he is, and doubtless you agree with me. So who but an idiot, I ask you, would commit murder with a weapon so easily identifiable as his property and leave it in his victim, thereby leading the law right to his door? The defence contends that the witnesses Ellis and Peter Wilton were *meant* to see what they saw. The murder scene was pre-chosen by a killer masquerading as Andrew Blake, the treacherous act staged for their benefit. Later in these proceedings, during my closing address, I will elaborate on the whole evil conspiracy, indicating the fact, not the possibility but the fact, that somebody else had a stronger motive than Andrew Blake and that Andrew Blake became a pawn in the game, a ready-made scapegoat. You will then,

I feel sure, deliver a verdict of not guilty."

"That concludes your address?" asked Ewing.

"Yes, Your Honor."

"Are you ready to call your witness?"

"Ready, Your Honor."

"Do so then."

Called to the stand, Slow Wolf, bareheaded but toting his battered beaver with its turkey feather adornment as though fearing it could be stolen, rose and plodded past lawmen and defendant, a portly, worried-looking redman drawing derisive chuckles from the body of the court. Ewing used his gavel and cold-eyed the offenders. I. P. Jeffries stepped forward to administer the oath.

"Take the bible in your left hand, raise your right hand. Do you swear to tell the truth, the whole truth and nothing but the truth? Say 'So help me, God'."

"So help me, God," mumbled Slow Wolf.

"State your name."

"Me Slow Wolf."

"Be seated."

Slow Wolf sat, sighed heavily and reflected,

'Now it begins — and will I be allowed keep my secret? This young one should be no problem but, of course, the prosecutor is bound to become difficult.'

"You have listened carefully to the words of the prosecution witnesses?" Marcus began. Slow Wolf nodded. "So you understand a man was killed the same night you first came to this town?" Another nod. "Please tell us what you did that night, starting from your arrival."

"Had deer-meat to trade," said Slow Wolf. "Rode along street to eating place, then go around back, knock on door."

"What eating place?"

"Blake's."

"How did you know it was the Blake cafe?"

"Read name out front."

"Continue, please."

"Man open door. We talk. He look at meat, give me wampum." Slow Wolf pointed to the defendant. "That man."

"What time was this?" asked Marcus.

"Ten," said Slow Wolf.

"Please tell us why you are sure of the time."

"Clock in room — behind man. I see it when I with him."

"We have to be certain about this, Slow Wolf, so tell us how you read time on the white man's clock."

"Short point on figures one and oh — ten. Long point on one and two — twelve."

"What did the clock show when you left Mister Blake?"

"Ten after ten."

"Did you stay here after selling venison to Mister Blake?"

"No. Camp by river."

"Thank you," nodded Marcus. "Your witness, Mister Alper."

Alper rose, advanced on the witness and eyed him sceptically.

"So you can read time by the white man's clocks?" he challenged. "Since when?" Before Slow Wolf could reply, he began haranguing him. "We all know how Indians read time, by the position of the sun during the day, by the moon and stars at night. You just happened to look at the clock in that kitchen? I put it to you that you have no interest in the white man's timepieces. You wouldn't know at *what* hour you were with the accused!"

"Objection," frowned Marcus. "Could my learned opponent refrain from confusing the witness? How, Your Honor, can this witness hope to answer questions when not given a chance to do so?"

"Point taken," said Ewing. "Mister Alper, while being argumentative, you put three questions. I presume you do wish him to answer?"

"I beg your forbearance, Your Honor." Alper made a fine show of righteous indignation, producing a handkerchief, wiping his forehead. "Though I've practised law many years, I can still be shocked. The wanton savagery of this vile deed, a fine young man struck down so mercilessly in only his twentieth year and now — as a defence witness — my young colleague produces a redskin . . . !"

"May I remind you I have ruled this witness as acceptable to the court," Ewing said sternly. "You've left it a little late to challenge my ruling, wouldn't you say? Carry on, please."

"Forgive me — I gave in to emotion," Alper apologized. "I believe I did, as you say, put three questions, but now I . . ."

"*My* emotions are under control," said Ewing. "You began, as I recall, by challenging the witness as to his ability to read time."

"Thank you, Your Honor, now I remember," nodded Alper, and he scowled at the witness and repeated his questions. "So you can read the white man's clocks?" Slow Wolf nodded calmly. "Since when?"

"Many moons," intoned Slow Wolf.

"And you just happened to look at the clock in the cafe kitchen?" snapped Alper.

"At ten of that clock," said Slow Wolf.

"You claim to understand the oath you took!" fumed Alper. "But how could you, an ignorant redskin, understand the meaning of the word perjury?" He gestured impatiently as Marcus rose to protest. "I am not threatening your precious witness, Counsellor. I should have used the term involuntary perjury — which I'm sure would be equally incomprehensible to him. To an Indian, one timepiece would look the same as any other." In a dramatic gesture, he whipped out his watch and held it to the witness's face. "What time do you read by my watch? Answer!"

Slow Wolf groaned inwardly, resenting what he was about to do, but feeling greater resentment of Alper's bullying. He replied clearly, his every word audible to a suddenly startled interrogator, judge, jury and all other parties present.

"It is ten-fifteen by your fine Waltham watch, Mister Prosecutor. This trial proceeds at a brisk pace. In one and a half hours, so much has been achieved, jury selection, yours and Mister Colley's opening addresses and the testimony of many witnesses heard. I am most impressed." There was a clattering sound. Ewing's gavel had slid from his grasp; the bailiff was on all fours, retrieving it for him. People were rising to gape at a redman expressing himself in excellent English. "As for my committing perjury, involuntary or otherwise, perish the thought, sir. To do so would be to incur the displeasure of this court and, worse still, break one of the Ten Commandments."

Stunned silence. First to rally, a red-faced Alper loudly appealed to a perplexed Judge Ewing.

"Your Honor, how *dare* the defence attorney resort to such disgraceful, underhand tactics! This witness is obviously a fake, a fraud, no Indian at all! The defence foolishly claims the killer was masquerading as the accused — while himself presenting an *obvious* masquerader! This rogue calling himself Slow Wolf could *not* be an Indian!"

To confirm this claim, he dashed to a table, saturated his handkerchief by upending a carafe and spilling a lot of water, then dashing back to the witness stand. As patiently as he was able, Slow Wolf submitted to the indignity of Alper's scrubbing at his swarthy visage. Uproar. Ewing quelled it with his gavel, stared hard at witness and prosecutor-turned-facewasher and said,

"I presume, Mister Alper, your handkerchief shows no trace of dye or greasepaint." Then he shifted his gaze to the astonished Marcus. "Counsellor, you owe us an explanation."

"I have no explanation, for I too am astounded," Marcus assured him. "You have my word that, until now, I had no idea Slow Wolf is so — erudite. In all our discussions, he used only broken English."

"That is true, Your Honor," offered Slow Wolf.

"Then *you* owe us an explanation," Ewing said accusingly.

"I fear so," agreed Slow Wolf. "And I believe I can convince you it was never my intention to cause offence — if you'll kindly direct Mister Alper to desist. I've never had my face washed in public before, and I find it most embarrassing."

"Mister Alper, please withdraw from the stand and compose yourself, while I question this man," ordered Ewing, and Alper obeyed, more confused than ever. "Now, Slow Wolf, you gave the first part of your testimony in the speech pattern we white people expect of an Indian with only a smattering of English. You then — admittedly under pressure — resorted to English of which a college professor might be proud. How is that possible?"

"An accident of birth," Slow Wolf said apologetically. "I am a half-breed. My father was a full-blood Sioux, my mother a white lady, a schoolteacher by profession. Having inherited my father's physical appearance, I am assumed to be a full-blood. And you, I've no doubt, have correctly assumed my dear mother — may she and my father rest in peace — tutored me as thoroughly as did he. To her I owe my above-average grounding in the English language, to him my knowledge of Indian lore, the skills of trapping hunting, etcetera."

"Such unpardonable deception!" interjected Alper.

"I haven't finished questioning him," growled Ewing. "And, Slow Wolf, you haven't finished explaining."

"Your Honor, if you'll forgive the liberty, try to imagine yourself in my situation," pleaded Slow Wolf. "Earlier in my years of wandering, I learned from bitter experience that a great many of my white brothers resent the anomaly, sometimes violently. Sadly, some frontier folk are poorly educated, some semi or completely illiterate. A redman expressing himself in fluent English is — just too much for them. They become furious. I have been expelled from innumerable frontier communities, assaulted most cruelly and, on one harrowing occasion, almost lynched. Life, believe me, can be extremely difficult for one whose appearance belies his gentle disposition and educational qualifications."

He shrugged and bowed his head. The court was hushed, so that the sound of a vehicle approaching along Main Street was clearly audible to all, including Stretch, who took no comfort from it; his ears were hopefully cocked for the hoofbeats of a saddle-horse, his partner's sorrel.

Ewing broke the silence by commenting, "Remarkable — and that's an understatement."

"But true, Your Honor," Slow Wolf

vowed, not raising his head. "I do realize I am still under oath."

"I accepted this man as a witness," Ewing told the prosecution and defence. "I also accept his revelations as to his origins. Mister Alper, you may resume cross-examination."

Fury and frustration got the better of Alper. He didn't question; he accused.

"Because the defendant dealt fairly with you, you felt a certain sympathy for him upon learning of his arrest and the time of the murder! I put it to you that you unloaded the venison on Blake some time *before* or *after* ten o'clock!"

"Sir, I do appreciate a fair price for whatever game I have to offer restaurateurs, storekeepers and other potential purchasers," replied Slow Wolf, "but not to the extreme you suggest. It was *ten* o'clock and, anticipating your next question, the clock had not stopped. I enjoy keen hearing. I heard it ticking. And, under no circumstances would I lie under oath. I do beg your pardon, but you and the jury just have to accept the fact that the defendant was not at the scene of the crime at that crucial time."

"Now I'm being lectured by this — this . . . !" blustered Alper.

"Objection sustained," nodded Ewing. "I should have interrupted the witness when his answer became a statement on behalf of the defence, but must confess I am still bemused by his excellent command of English."

"I have no more questions," scowled Alper, turning his back on Slow Wolf.

"You may step down," Ewing said and, as Slow Wolf quit the witness stand, he eyed defence counsel enquiringly. "Only the one defence witness, I believe, Mister Colley?"

Marcus happened to be glancing at the taller Texan at this moment. He saw Stretch turn and half-rise, his homely visage creasing in a grin of relief.

"May I have a moment, Your Honor,

just a moment?" He rose, glimpsed the two new arrivals in muttered conference with Dan Fox in the court-house entrance, one tall, burly and familiar, the other shorter and a stranger, then patted Blake's shoulder encouragingly. "At least one more witness for the defence, I think."

"You mean you aren't sure?" challenged Ewing.

"Yeah, Judge, he's sure," called Larry.

And now he began a slow progress down the centre aisle, baring his head. He had discarded the cane and, to Stretch's alarm, limped and winced. The nod he aimed at Marcus was eloquent, and Marcus gratefully announced,

"I call, as my next witness, Lawrence Valentine."

Larry was barely half-way along the aisle when a grim-faced Gil Heisler rose and, followed by his four companions, began leaving. By prearrangement with Larry, Fox made no move to impede them. Hat in hand, Henri Colbert made for a vacated seat.

For the rest of his journey to the witness stand, Larry was under close scrutiny; he had no doubt the judge had recognized him, or knew him by reputation. Jeffries administered the oath. Larry made hard work of seating himself and then, to Alper's disapproval, crooked a finger at Marcus, who approached him eagerly.

"Your Honor." Alper stood up. "I'm as familiar with this witness's reputation as you no doubt are. He is a drifter, an adventurer, a . . . "

"A troubleshooter," interjected Ed Gaskell, grinning with his pencil poised. "And quite an investigator. Alan Pinkerton himself tried to hire him."

"If interruptions cease, we may hear the remainder of the defence's case before we break for lunch," Ewing said sourly.

"Sorry, Judge," shrugged Gaskell.

"You have an objection, Mister Alper?" challenged Ewing. "So soon?

The witness has not yet begun his testimony."

Alper took the hint and resumed his seat. And now, by the skillful phrasing of his first question, Marcus won the judge's full attention; and Ewing wasn't the only one.

"Will you explain to the court the relevance of your journey to Polvadera as it relates to this trial?"

Larry glanced at the jurors and answered the question with a question.

"You talked about Andy Blake's coat yet?"

"Now, really, Your Honor . . ." protested Alper.

"It's irregular, but this witness has only now arrived," said Ewing. "I'm going to answer the witness's question on the assumption that it relates to the testimony we are about to hear. Mister Valentine, defence counsel has raised the argument that the murderer of Judson Daneman could have disguised himself as the accused."

"Much obliged, Judge," acknowledged

Larry. "All right now, here's how it goes. I learned from Mrs Blake that Andy bought his checkered coat, the only one of its kind in town, from a tailor in Polvadera, so I travelled there to find that tailor — his name's Henry Colbert and he's right here now — and find out if he sold another coat, exactly like Andy's, just recent."

"And . . . ?" asked Marcus.

Larry paused to watch a man rise and retreat to the entrance. He had anticipated Nader or Staley would now make a hasty departure. Well, this one, the lawyer handling Box D's legal affairs, just happened to be of a height with Andy Blake. Well, well, well. Harley Forbes hurried out. Dan Fox maintained his post just inside the courtroom entrance, but the other deputy moved. Thursby's curiosity was aroused; he too made a hasty departure. Stretch hesitated a moment, then quit his seat to join Fox for a muttered exchange of questions and answers.

"And?" Marcus asked again.

216

"And he did," said Larry. "Made a coat the same size, same checkered cloth, in just one day. A woman gave him the order and the measurements too."

"Were you able to establish the identity of the woman?" prodded Marcus.

"The Box D widow, Mrs Daneman," said Larry. "Henry identified her from a newspaper picture I showed him, and he's here to swear to it if you want." He glanced at the jury again and brought Alper to his feet with another question to Marcus. "You talk to 'em about somebody stealin' one of Andy's knives?"

Before Alper could give voice to his objection, Ewing told Larry,

"The defence has raised that point." He noted Larry shifting in his chair, wincing again. "Are you in pain?"

"Some," nodded Larry. "Got ambushed after I quit Polvadera, stopped a slug and had to double back to have it dug out, else I'd've got here in time to give Marcus what I'd learned." He grinned mirthlessly. "Seems somebody figures I've learned too much."

"Isn't it now obvious my point is proven, Your Honor?" challenged Marcus. "There were others conspiring to murder Jud Daneman, others with strong motives . . ."

"Save it for the jury, Mister Colley," chided Ewing. "You are still examining your witness."

"Who has certainly enlightened us," Marcus said cheerfully. "Anything to add, Larry — I mean Mister Valentine?"

"Nothin' I can think of," said Larry. "But don't forget the tailor, huh? Henry Colbert's the name."

"Thank you," said Marcus. "Your witness, Mister Prosecutor."

Alper rose, studied Larry a long moment, then told the judge,

"No questions of this witness — but I'll have several for the tailor from Polvadera."

Permitted to leave the stand, Larry

did so with some effort. Stretch came to his side and supported him up the aisle to a rear seat where they were joined by Fox, who grinned smugly and muttered,

"Too bad you stopped one. But, just like I figured, you're bustin' this case, amigo. *Bustin'* it!"

Marcus called the tailor to the stand. Jeffries administered the oath, after which Colbert seated himself, flicked a speck from the lapel of his smart jacket and smiled invitingly at Marcus.

"Just a few questions, Mister Colbert."

"I'm at your disposal, sir."

"Having fashioned both coats, the one sold to the defendant some years ago, the one made to the specifications of Mrs Daneman just recently, can you say they were identical?"

"Give or take an inch here and there, absolutely. The same material, you see. A distinctive check pattern."

"And there is no doubt in your mind as to the identity of the purchaser?"

"None at all."

"You were required to devote an entire day to making that garment. Is this customary?"

"No. Usually, I have the client in my store. I take his measurements and begin cutting. By appointment, he returns for a first fitting of the half-constructed garment. It can take several days, or a week or more, depending on my work load and the availability of the client. It *is* unusual for another party to supply a list of measurements and offer to pay extra for completion of a coat in just one day but, of course, I managed it."

"Will you look at the defendant — do you mind rising, Mister Blake?"

The defendant rose. He was, of course, wearing the coat so familiar to his family, friends, neighbors, just about the entire Vista Ford population.

"We meet again, Mister Blake," Colbert remarked. "My regrets that it should be under such unhappy circumstances. Still a comfortable fit, the coat?"

"Feels fine, Mister Colbert, and doesn't even look like wearing out," said Blake. "Thanks for coming all the way from Polvadera."

"The social niceties," jibed Alper, "A diversion from the business at hand, the hearing of testimony."

"Mister Colley, if you please," frowned Ewing.

"Yes, Your Honor," said Marcus. "Mister Colbert, do you identify the defendant as the purchaser of the garment he now wears?"

"At my store some three years ago," nodded Colbert. "He is Mister Andrew Blake, in Polvadera at that time to visit his indisposed cousin, Nathan Greeley."

The defendant resumed his seat and Marcus turned his witness over to the prosecution. By now, Alper was mentally reviewing the case and experiencing doubts; nothing seemed as clear-cut any more. But he still had a job to do.

"The pattern of the jacket worn by

the defendant, is it really so rare? I acknowledge you as well-qualified to answer the question, since clothing is your business."

"Gents' apparel, to be specific," said Colbert. "The pattern in question is referred to in the trade as hound's tooth. Usually, the checks are smaller. Rare? Not in big cities, I'd imagine, but mine is the only store in Polvadera at which the particular fabric and pattern is available. And, according to my friend, Mister Valentine, no store in this town stocks it."

"I'm sure the court would be interested to know how you could so positively identify Mrs Arlene Daneman," frowned Alper. "Were you already acquainted? Had the lady visited Polvadera previously?"

"I had never seen her before," said Colbert. "As to whether she had been in town on other occasions, I just wouldn't know."

"Then, by what means could you . . . ?"

222

"Mister Valentine showed me a photograph. Front page of the Platt County *Post*."

The editor of that publication looked up, mumbled something under his breath and resumed scribbling. Ed Gaskell's excitement was increasing by the minute, he was anticipating record sales of a special edition featuring his coverage of the trial.

"Newspaper photographs are a poor likeness at best," argued Alper. "Plainly, the defence is making an issue of this matter so you must realize, Mister Colbert, the accuracy of this identification is of the utmost importance."

"I do realize that," Colbert assured him. "And, excuse me, but newspaper photographs often present an excellent likeness. If I may quote an example, the picture of Mister Valentine and his friend Mister Emerson."

"If it — uh — please the court," said Gaskell, rising. "And begging Your Honor's pardon . . . "

"Make it brief," ordered Ewing.

"I consider the picture of Mrs Daneman published in my last edition to be a perfect likeness," offered Gaskell. "And nobody else, including the lady herself, has said otherwise. Just trying to help, Your Honor."

He sat and retrieved his pencil. But Alper wasn't giving up without a struggle.

"Are you absolutely certain the lady who gave you those measurements . . . ?" he began.

"I wasn't," interjected Colbert. "That is, not at first."

"Ah hah!" Alper's eyes gleamed. "Now, sir, exactly what is *that* supposed to mean?"

Ewing had to gavel for silence; the onlookers were reacting too audibly for his liking.

"These interruptions are trying my patience," he warned everybody. "Witness, you'll answer the question."

"Mister Valentine showed me the newspaper picture of a quite beautiful blonde lady," Colbert patiently explained.

"She bore no apparent resemblance to the lady who ordered the jacket. You see, on that occasion, she was in disguise, pretending to be a high-class Mexican lady."

"This is hearsay at best!" accused Alper. "You are under oath to give direct answers, not to venture personal opinions!"

"This *is* a direct answer, sir," declared Colbert. "Mister Valentine sketched in a few details, showed me the picture again and I at once recognized her as the woman calling herself Senora de Cordoba and affecting a Mexican accent." He reached into a pocket. "I have the cutting right here — see for yourself."

Alper exploded into what could only be described as an ecstasy of scorn. Marcus got to his feet and insisted Ewing inspect the clipping. He and Alper were into a heated argument until Ewing demanded they approach the bench; Gaskell dared the judge's wrath by joining the two lawyers.

Getting in the first word, Marcus insisted,

"It's not as outlandish as it at first seems, Your Honor. The lady in question used to be an actress."

"I'm aware of that," scowled Alper.

"*I* was *not*," Ewing said testily.

"We aren't discussing an impossibility," muttered Marcus, as Ewing studied the altered picture, seemingly unaware Gaskell had ascended to the bench and was squinting over his shoulder. "Your Honor, I'm deeply committed to the proposition that my client does have an alibi and that there can be only one explanation for the testimony of the Wilton brothers. The man they saw was masquerading as Andrew Blake and . . . "

"And Mrs Daneman *could* pass for a Mexican," interjected Gaskell. "Judge, an actress, could get away with it. All it'd take is a black wig — and I've just remembered she's dark-eyed. And faking a Mex accent? Dead easy for her."

"But, confound it, Valentine darkening the hair and eyebrows with a pencil," protested Alper. "Can we accept that?"

"What is more important here?" demanded Marcus. "Justice for the accused, or a tenacious clinging to due procedure?"

"Don't make a distinction, young man," muttered Ewing. "*Both* are important." He checked his watch. "Now, gentlemen, here's how I see it." Grimacing, he nudged Gaskell. "If your backside isn't in your seat in ten seconds I'll find you in contempt." The newspaperman hastily returned to his seat. "This is how we'll proceed. If you're through with this witness, Mister Alper, we'll adjourn for lunch and reconvene at — let's say a quarter of two. You'll then make your closing address during which you'll have ample opportunity to discredit the evidence obtained by the witness Valentine. After that, it will be your turn, Mister Marcus. And, if both of you can resist the urge to orate at great length — who knows? — the jury may retire by mid-afternoon."

Colbert was allowed stand down. Ewing warned the jury against discussion of the case during the lunch break, announcing the adjournment and the courtroom emptied. Blake was allowed a few words with his wife and daughters before being escorted back to the county jail by the sheriff.

And Larry, Stretch and Deputy Fox were in conference in front of a livery stable, standing by three saddle horses.

"I can't talk you out of it?" Fox challenged Larry.

"I've done all I can for Andy," growled Larry. "Now I got a score to settle with that sonofabitch Heisler."

8

Justice for All

THE burly deputy wasn't through pleading.

"I've gone along with you up to now," he pointed out. "Sure, I don't forget I got you jaspers into this thing and, just like I expected, you've given Andy a better chance than he had before. I didn't stop Heisler and his buddies from leavin', and that was your idea, Larry . . ."

"Headed back to Box D you said," recalled Larry, inspecting the chestnut his partner had rented for him.

"You made one of them ambushers tell you it was Heisler ordered you killed," said Fox. "And that makes it law business."

"Where's the Chief?" Larry asked Stretch.

"Back in Dan's room," said Stretch. "He'll be in court again after lunch, count on that."

"Well, he's done all his testifyin', so nobody's gonna crowd him now, him or Marcus," opined Larry.

"Will you for Pete's sake *listen* to me?" growled Fox. "You got a leg wound. You're in no shape for bracin' Heisler. Try ridin' out there and . . . "

"I'll be forkin' the chestnut," Larry said bluntly. "Ain't fixin' to travel to a showdown in a sprung rig. Not my style."

"Heisler's a fast gun, got a reputation," warned Fox.

"Thanks for tellin' me," said Larry, grinning coldly.

"Meanin' what?" frowned Fox.

"I know his kind," said Larry. "If I hit him dead centre, I'd be doin' him a favor, and its for sure I owe him no favors." As Fox made to speak again, he planted his left palm against his chest. "Dan, stay out of this. I'm not tryin' to boss you around. I'm askin' you as a friend."

Stretch gave him a boost, then swung astride his pinto. The Texans departed slowly, making for the trail that would take them to Box D range. Staring after them, Fox lit a cigar, did some fast and fancy cussing and muttered aloud,

"The hell I'll stay out of it."

The other deputy, meanwhile, was seething with curiosity, also excited, convinced he would soon cover himself in glory. Following Harley Forbes out of town and on to Daneman land, he had spared no thought for others he'd seen headed in that direction. Heisler and his four sidekicks were forgotten. Thursby was concentrating only on the lawyer, remembering how Forbes had dashed to his office, emerged immediately afterward toting a valise and then rented a saddle animal.

His vantagepoint was a rise on Box D range. He squatted atop it, watching the ranch headquarters. Moments before, he had seen the lawyer dismount in the front yard and speak briefly with a hired hand before hustling into the house. Now the Box D surrey stood in readiness, two handsome charcoals in harness.

'What it means is somebody's takin' a trip and maybe they don't plan on comin' back,' be decided. 'And why would they do that, what're they runnin' from?'

He had always been pro-Box D, acknowledging the power of the Daneman name. But this was a time for second thoughts. Did it have to be Blake stabbed young Jud? Maybe not. Hell, all the killer needed was a coat like Blake's.

His excitement increased when Forbes emerged from the ranch-house hefting valises which he tossed into the surrey. Then Arlene Daneman appeared, dressed for travelling. The lawyer helped her up to the front seat, climbed up beside her and took the reins and, at speed, the vehicle moved.

'Northwest,' Thursby noted. 'By damn, they're makin' for high country and, after they reach that mountain trail, they could be out of Platt County in a couple hours — but not before they do some explainin'.

He retreated to his waiting horse, remounted and began following the fast-moving surrey. Soon, he was spurring his mount to a gallop, because Forbes was driving those blacks like a man possessed.

Forty-five minutes later, urging his animal up a steep ascent, he resisted the impulse to glance to his left. To do so would be to invite vertigo. He knew this part of the mountains, didn't need to remind himself that, beyond the outer edge, there was nothing; the trail just fell away to a precipice, deep, its near face sheer and dotted with outcroppings of brush and rock. He hugged the inside of the trail, finished the climb, rounded a bend and hastily drew rein.

The surrey was stalled a short distance ahead, the woman still seated, Forbes standing beside the vehicle, spelling the team, talking to her until he spotted Thursby.

The ambitious deputy nudged his mount to movement again, advancing slowly, calling,

"You folks're in a big hurry, seems like."

Forbes offered no rejoinder. What he did do made Thursby's scalp crawl. From under his coat, the lawyer drew a pistol, aimed and fired. And, unlike two certain Texans, Ray Thursby had never suffered the nerve-shattering feel of a bullet missing his head with only an inch to spare, of actually feeling its wind. As he gasped and keeled sideways, he caught a fleeting glimpse of the lawyer's tense expression, of Arlene Daneman glaring back at him. The ground rushed up to meet him. He fell heavily as his mount reared, and then he was rolling in frantic haste, fearful Forbes would fire again and with greater accuracy.

But there was no second shot. Forbes had obeyed the irate woman and reboarded the vehicle. When Thursby sat up, still in shock, the surrey was moving again, the lawyer whipping the blacks to speed.

On *this* trail? That was Thursby's thought as he lurched upright and stumbled to his quivering horse. In the saddle or driving any kind of vehicle, this winding route through the mountains could only be travelled at a cautious pace; every citizen of the county knew that. He remounted to resume the pursuit. Holy Moses, the lawyer and the widow were fleeing in panic. This was no pleasure trip; it was a getaway, so they obviously had plenty to fear from the law. If he could head them off, arrest Forbes for the attempted murder of a deputy sheriff — hell! He'd be the number one lawman of Platt County and a certainty to defeat Kepple come election-time!

He rounded that bend and another to ride a fairly straight section of the high trail, the surrey visible some distance ahead, still going too fast for safety in these conditions.

The vehicle disappeared around another curve and, moments later, the ominous sounds smote his ears and he began sweating — the frightened cries of the black teamers, the woman's scream of horror. Apprehensively, he kept his mount to the inside of the trail and slowed on his way to that bend.

It was a harrowing scene. His breath caught in his throat when he turned the bend and jerked his horse to a halt. The surrey had overturned by the outer edge and was on its side, its rightside wheels spinning, the blacks nickering in alarm, trapped in their harness. He swung down and moved to the edge, not afoot but on hands and knees and, when he stared over and downward, wished he hadn't. He would never forget what he now saw. The bodies were still falling, the baggage too. A valise struck an outjutting rock, burst open and careered out over the yawning chasm, pieces of clothing scattering. Then, abruptly, the bodies were lost from view; there was no way the runaways could survive.

His clothes clinging to him, saturated with sweat, he edged a safe distance from the rim before rising. And it was then he heard another vehicle. It was approaching from the opposite direction and slowly; he could bet a month's pay the driver of this *rig* was in familiar territory and treating it with due respect for his own welfare.

He recognized the wagon with its gaily painted canopy. Peddler Josh Hammett marketed his wares three or four times per year in Platt County, much to the indignation of the merchants of Vista Ford, all of whom regarded him as unfair competition. To ingratiate himself with local businessmen, Thursby had barred the peddler from the county seat so that, nowadays, he did business only at outlying ranches and homesteads. Hammett had good reasons for disliking Thursby, but now Thursby was glad to see him. He was making hard work of calming the distressed blacks, and Hammett happened to be a man of powerful physique.

"Lend a hand!" he pleaded, as the peddler stalled his rig. "I need all the help I can get to raise the surrey — onto all four wheels . . . !"

"Lord Almighty!" Hammett dropped from his seat, gaping. "What about . . . ?"

"Two of 'em — man and woman!" panted Thursby. "I didn't see 'em overturn, not from the other side of the bend, but plain enough he — took it too fast. Oh, hell! I saw 'em . . . "

"Rig's right close to the edge," Hammett observed, his voice shaking. "They — uh — went over?"

"Still fallin' when — I peeked over the edge," mumbled Thursby.

They managed to soothe the team. It took their combined strength, sweating, straining with their muscles aching in protest, to force the vehicle back onto its wheels. The peddler inspected the reins and harness, still pacifying the team, while Thursby checked the wheels and decided the surrey could roll again.

"Didn't bust a spoke or an axle, huh?" frowned Hammett. "Well, that's a wonderment. All right now, I'm not as jumpy as you, so it better be me turns the team. You'll be taking the rig back to Vista Ford?"

"And you can follow me in if you want," nodded Thursby. "I'll tie my horse in back and drive it to town."

"I'm barred from Vista Ford," Hammett sourly reminded him.

"Not any more," said Thursby. "I owe you. Couldn't've righted the surrey without your help and I'm not too proud to admit I'm leery of turnin' that team."

Hammett did it with care, being himself demoralized by the proximity of the precipice. Well under control now, the blacks were guided in a half-circle with their heads southeast, after which the deputy tied his mount behind, waited for the peddler to return to his own vehicle, then climbed to the surrey's front seat and gathered the reins. His return to Vista Ford began.

The Texans, at this time, were following the trail toward Box D range, but taking their time, out of deference to Larry's wound. Stretch drawled a good-humored jibe. He just couldn't resist reminding his partner,

"You're the one don't never turn me loose by myself, always claiming I run into strife soon as we're separated."

"Rub it in," invited Larry. "Have your fun."

"So off you went, headed all the way to Polvadera," Stretch continued. "Played detective, proved the real killer was rigged in a jacket just like Andy's, got everything you needed — then started back and rid smack-dab into an ambush with me not there to back you up."

"I do dumb things sometimes," shrugged Larry.

Stretch waxed serious. "You hurtin', runt?"

"It smarts some," said Larry. "After

I pay Heisler off for settin' them bushwhackers onto me, we'll go back to town and I'll flop, while you find me a doc. Bandage likely needs changin'."

In the distance, they heard the lowing of cattle warning them they had almost reached Box D land. They stopped talking, suddenly leery of the terrain they now rode, rock clusters to their left, a copse to their right, a bend dead ahead. Well, Dan Fox had done as they demanded. Gil Heisler and his four companions had been allowed quit the courthouse. Larry had assumed the five would retreat to the ranch headquarters; now he wondered if he had guessed right. No special reason, just the tingling of his short hairs.

Softly, he warned his partner.

"Remember, whatever happens from here on, Heisler's mine."

"You're welcome," replied Stretch. "If we don't find him alone, if his gunhung companeros're around, I'll be watchin' 'em real careful."

On their approach to the bend, they

slowed their mounts to a walk, Larry warily scanning the trees to their right, Stretch keeping an eye on the rocks. They rounded the bend and drew rein.

Twenty-five yards separated them from the four men blocking their path, Heisler and three of his sidekicks, no sign of the fifth man. They stood in a line, Heisler's face tense, the other men impassive. The nicker of a horse beyond a patch of brush indicated they had left their horses there.

"Been expectin' you, Valentine," growled Heisler.

Larry nodded coolly. He and Stretch dismounted. A gentle slap to the withers was all it took to start their animals plodding away from them.

"Well, sure," said Larry. "Knew I'd come lookin' for you, right? I stopped a bullet when three of your no-good buddies bushwhacked me. You didn't count on seein' me again, but here I am hero."

"Figurin' you got a score to settle," guessed Heisler.

"I didn't kill 'em all," Larry grimly informed him. "The one I winged didn't much appreciate my iron proddin' his ear. That's how I know it was you sent 'em after me."

"Stayin' in Polvadera would've been healthier," scowled Heisler. "You and your scrawny friend've lived too long, meddled too often, butted into too many things that were none of your business."

"Pardon us all to hell," drawled Stretch. "It's this old notion we can't shake off, a man hangin' for what he didn't do."

"Bothers you, huh?" Larry challenged Heisler. He had to let his right leg support his weight, an awkward stance, but he was ready for anything, as would be learned by the first man to make a wrong move. "You'd as soon Blake hung anyway?"

"Don't care a damn either way." snapped Heisler. "If Blake can prove he didn't knife Jud, that's fine for him."

"Couldn't've been you?" prodded Larry.

"That kid was like a son to me!" cried Heisler.

"You still got trouble, Heisler," declared Larry. "When a man sets me up for an ambush, he answers for it to me — or to the law. Conspiracy to murder, they call it. Your choice, Heisler. You unstrap your hogleg and surrender . . . " One of Heisler's companions laughed scathingly, "or you make your play, which would be one helluva mistake."

There would be no surrender, not voluntarily anyway. He could tell from the expression in Heisler's eyes. And Heisler was a potentially deadly adversary, one of the fastest Larry had ever gone up against. His Colt cleared leather at speed, but a shade slower than Larry's.

With the roar of Larry's .45, the other three filled their hands, but no faster than Stretch's matched Colts were out and booming and wreaking havoc. Heisler wasn't given time to pull trigger. He was lurching backward and loosing a wail of agony, his gun dropping from nerveless fingers, his right arm a bloody mess. Discharging his pistols, Stretch sent one man reeling and another to the dust, there to writhe in his death-throes. The fourth man had a clear bead on Stretch when, from somewhere behind and left of him, another six-gun roared. The fourth man was dead before he collapsed.

Because Heisler was helpless now, Larry could afford to shift his gaze. He raised his left arm, recocked and steadied his Colt's barrel on his forearm as the fifth man rose above the rocks ahead and to the left. He was levelling a shotgun the double load from which could have struck both trouble-shooters, but for Larry's unwavering accuracy. His Colt roared again. The shotgunner shuddered, twisted and nosedived from atop the rock, his weapon discharging into the ground seconds before he hit it.

"All right, that's all of 'em." The familiar voice reached the Texans from somewhere to their rear, along with the approaching footsteps. "And you don't have to thank me."

"We thank you anyway, Dan," grinned Stretch. Larry left it to his partner and the deputy to check on the other men. He made straight for where Heisler had dropped, still conscious, groaning in anguish. Fox, after discovering they'd be taking three dead and two wounded gunmen back to Vista Ford, moved forward to join Larry. Incapable of lowering himself to a half-kneeling position, Larry stared down into Heisler's contorted face.

"Why?" he demanded. "Why'd you have to offer them bushwhackers a hundred apiece to kill me?"

"It was her!" gasped Heisler.

"Meanin'?" frowned Fox.

"Arlene . . . !" groaned Heisler. "I don't know why. She — just said for me to — set it up — and I'd've done *anything* for her — *anything* . . . !"

Fox studied Heisler's wrecked and bleeding arm and said, grimacing,

"Some mess — some helluva mess."

"Like I said," Larry grimly reminded him, "I could've hit him dead-centre, but I owed him no favors."

"I don't know if you'll end up one-armed, Heisler," said Fox. "What I *do* know is you'll be many a long year in a territorial prison. Larry, Stretch, it's anybody's guess whether we'll deliver this trash before the trial's over, but we gotta try."

Marcus, at this moment, was rounding off his closing address to the jury, his the only voice to be heard in the packed courtroom. Seated not far from the sheriff, the defendant and the county attorney, Slow Wolf kept his eyes on the young lawyer and his ears cocked; he was as inscrutable as ever, but keenly approving Marcus's forceful delivery.

'Excellent,' he reflected. 'Enunciation far superior to his opponent's, the jury in the palm of his hand. Every relevant point duly stressed — and without extravagant rhetoric. Ah, yes. This young man will go far in his chosen profession.'

"Beyond a reasonable doubt, gentlemen of the jury," Marcus emphasized. "To arrive at a verdict of guilty, it is imperative you have *no* doubt that my client committed the treacherous crime of which he stands accused. But the weight of the evidence you have heard is unchallengeably in his favour — you *have* to doubt his guilt. In your deliberations, remember the testimony of Slow Wolf, the witness we now know to be only half-Sioux and a man of perception, integrity and formidable intelligence. The prosecution failed to sway him. He was there in the cafe kitchen — with the accused — at the time of the murder. Remember too the evidence offered by the witnesses Valentine and Colbert — proof positive that the *real* murderer of Judson Daneman went to pains to impersonate the defendant. Everything

248

you've heard, the disappearance of one of the defendant's knives, the fact that the Wilton brothers did not see the face of the killer, must lead you to the conclusion the killer *was* a masquerader and my client his *second* victim. First the deceased — for whatever motive — then the accused — a convenient scapegoat. And so I put it to you that the only just verdict you can deliver is *not guilty*."

Plainly, he had spellbound the crowd. In the body of the court, a local began clapping, but subsided when the judge glared at him and banged his gavel. Marcus traded smiles with an entranced Linda and made for the seat beside his client's. Ewing cleared his throat.

"My summing up will be brief," he announced. "It is the duty of a presiding judge to clarify pertinent details of the case so that the jury will properly appreciate its responsibility. However, in his closing address, counsel for the defence seems to have anticipated major points of my summation." He paused, frowning in disapproval. A wild-eyed Deputy Thursby had returned, and noisily. He was running, not walking, down the centre aisle, shedding trail-dust. "Deputy, this is unacceptable behaviour! A judge cannot be interrupted during his . . . !"

"Has — the jury voted?" demanded Thursby, as he reached the bench.

"The jury has not retired to consider its verdict," said Ewing. "I am beginning my summation."

"Somethin's happened!" panted Thursby. "I got to tell you — because — I'm sure it ties in with the case!" He raised his voice above the rumble of comment from the body of the court, excitedly recounting his tailing of Harley Forbes to Box D and the swift leavetaking of the lawyer and the widow in the surrey, then his pursuit, his near-death at Forbes's hands and the ensuing chase along the mountain trail. "And — when I turned that bend, the rig was on its side. Everything in it — and *them* — meanin' Forbes and

250

Arlene Daneman — got thrown off the edge. Oh, hell! I saw 'em fallin'!"

His voice choked off. He back-stepped, trembling, to sag into the chair hastily vacated by Alper, who approached the bench with Marcus at his heels.

"I don't know what to say, Your Honor," muttered the prosecutor. "This unexpected turn of events . . . "

"Without precedent, I'd imagine," offered Marcus. "It obviously has bearing on the case, Your Honor."

"But all testimony has been heard, and you're summing up," said Alper.

"Gentlemen, I don't need to be told we have a quandary here," sighed Ewing. He dug out a kerchief, mopped at his face and dropped his voice to a near-whisper to confide, "What I need desperately — right now — is a good stiff belt of whiskey."

"I won't add to the confusion by requesting your permission to address the jury again," Marcus assured him. "As well as being irregular, it would be superfluous. They heard everything the deputy said."

"I can only suggest, if I may take the liberty," said Alper, "that you'll have to include some remark about the deputy's shock revelation."

"I could hardly sidestep it," agreed Ewing. "Very well, I'll continue." The lawyers retreated, Marcus to his seat, Alper to perch on the edge of the table at which the sheriff and defendant sat. Again, Ewing cleared his throat. "A startling announcement indeed," he remarked to the jury. "As it seems hardly likely the deputy invented what he has told us, or imagined it, we have to conclude the flight and violent demise of the deceased's stepmother and — uh — her companion — is of some significance."

He paused, his jaw sagging. He didn't want to believe it but, *yes*, it was happening again. The second of Kepple's deputies had barged through the street entrance, and not alone. Tagged by the taller trouble shooter, he came striding down the aisle to the bench.

"Judge, you gotta hear this before Andy's sentenced!" growled Fox. "Sorry for bustin' in like this, but it's important!"

"Get it said then," Ewing urged and, in exasperation, he tossed his gavel over his shoulder, propped his elbows and cupped his chin in his hands. "Go ahead, Deputy. I needn't assure you you have our undivided attention."

"On his way back from Polvadera, after he found out that Widow Daneman bought a jacket just like Andy's, Larry Valentine was ambushed . . ." began Fox.

"We know that, Fox," Alper said impatiently. "Get to your point."

"The Box D man Larry wounded — he's laid up in the Polvadera calaboose now — told Larry it was the ramrod, Heisler, offered 'em a hundred apiece to make sure Larry never made it back here alive," declared Fox. "Well, Larry and his partner here, they headed for Box D for a showdown after we broke for lunch. I tailed 'em and saw everything — heard everything too. Heisler and four of his buddies started a gunfight . . . "

"Dan had to get into it," interjected Stretch.

"We just got back," finished Fox. "Three stiffs we dropped off at Hawtrey's, two wounded we stashed in the county jail. Gil Heisler's talked, and who d'you suppose ordered him to choose three gun-toters to go ambush Larry?"

"I don't *have* to suppose, Deputy." Ewing said tartly. "You're about to tell us."

"Mrs Daneman!" announced Fox. "Now, damn it, that's gotta mean somethin', don't it?"

Ewing didn't regret having discarded his gavel; he doubted a gunshot could have quelled the uproar following Fox's statement. Blake was on his feet, trading waves and smiles with his womenfolk. Linda Colley had left her seat and was hugging her husband. Locals were loudly airing opinions. In his excitement Ed Gaskell had broken the point of his pencil and was pleading frantically for a replacement or at least a knife. And the twelve good men and true? The jury box was buzzing, the dozen jurymen conferring among themselves, pointing to Blake and both deputies, nodding emphatically.

The foreman of the jury finally won silence by bellowing to Ewing. Suddenly, the people were quiet, watching, waiting.

"Judge, we figure we've heard enough, so is it okay if we give a . . . ?"

"Are you saying the jury has already reached its verdict?" demanded Ewing. The foreman nodded eagerly. "A moment, if you please. Remain standing, but don't speak yet." He heaved a sigh and crooked a finger. Alper approached. Marcus disengaged himself from his wife's embrace and followed. To ensure only the attorneys would hear him, he leaned over the bench; they pressed themselves against its front, staring up at him, "Mister Alper, as county attorney, you're entitled to . . . "

"I know what you're going to say, Your Honor," muttered Alper. "Several options open to me, such as a lengthy protest about the disruptions, a demand the jury be replaced, but why prolong the agony for Blake — and everybody else?"

"In the final analysis, justice is what counts," declared Marcus. Ewing frowned at him incredulously. "Sorry. No impertinence intended. I'd *never* imply you need reminding."

"Thanks, son," Ewing said wearily. "Well, Mister Alper?"

"It couldn't be the first time in legal history a jury made its decision without retiring," shrugged Alper. "I've guessed their verdict. In the light of what transpired during the luncheon adjournment, how else could they vote? So, if you decide to hear the decision now, the prosecution has no objection." He turned to Marcus. "I should do you the courtesy of asking . . . "

"I appreciate the courtesy, sir," said Marcus. "But I believe we've both guessed the verdict."

"That makes three of us," said Ewing. "All right, you may withdraw." Marcus and Alper withdrew. He slumped in his padded chair and eyed the jury foreman again. "You have indicated the jury has reached a verdict. Is the verdict unanimous?"

"Sure is, Judge," nodded the foreman.

"Very well, you may announce your verdict," invited Ewing.

"We find Andy Blake not guilty," grinned the foreman.

Ewing waited for the cheering to cease. He then mopped his brow again and announced,

"The prisoner is discharged from custody. Sheriff Kepple, clear the court."

Stretch joined the jubilant Blakes long enough to shake hands with the cafeowner and be hugged by Irma and her daughters before joining the departing throng. It was then that a brown hand tugged at his shirtsleeve.

"Woodville, what of Lawrence?"

"He's fine, Chief," grinned Stretch, hooking an arm about Slow Wolf's plump shoulders. "Dan and me delivered the stiffs and the prisoners and I sent a doc name of Elcott to our room at Sanford's. Larry just figured he ought to rest up and have the doc fix him a clean bandage. C'mon, we'll go check on him."

"Just long enough to say goodbye," Slow Wolf insisted, as they emerged from the courthouse. "For reasons which I'm sure you've guessed, I feel I should flee this town without delay."

"You got nothin' to fret about," soothed Stretch. "Did your duty, didn't you? Folks admire you for that."

"Some, perhaps," said Slow Wolf. "But, to most, I'm an oddity akin to a sideshow freak and, inevitably, there'll be many goaded to jealousy by my use of the language they speak so poorly."

The doctor had left when they arrived. Larry was taking it easy, figuring he had earned his rest. Try as they might, neither he nor his partner could persuade the pudgy half-breed to prolong his stay. So, for the trouble-shooters and a valued friend, it was a typical farewell, no long speeches.

"May the Great Spirit protect you, my white brothers," Slow Wolf intoned. "Though our paths may never cross again . . ."

"Bull," grinned Larry. "We're always runnin' into you. Ride safe, Chief."

"Be seein' you, ol' buddy," Stretch said affectionately.

Slow Wolf was at the livery stable. He had readied his horse and was about to mount when Deputy Fox came ambling in. The burly deputy grinned broadly and grasped his hand.

"Sure surprised this town, didn't you? Ain't you the strangest Injun of all? High-falutin', plumb educated."

"I should apologize, Deputy Fox, for having deceived you," Slow Wolf said penitently. "But there are reasons why I . . . !"

"Forget it," shrugged Fox. "Larry and Stretch explained it — in lingo I could savvy. Well, so-long, amigo. And, if we ever meet again, you don't have to call me Deputy or Mister. I'm Dan to my friends."

"Most amiable of you," acknowledged Slow Wolf.

"My pleasure," said Fox. "Well? Ain't you gonna tell me your *front* name?"

"I have two," said Slow Wolf. "My full name is Cathcart Pettigrew Slow Wolf."

Fox winced.

"Cathcart — Pet . . . ?" He shook his head. "Too rich for my blood. So-long — Slow Wolf."

At sundown, the street door of Blake's Cafe was locked, a sign in the window reading 'Reopening For Breakfast.' All four Blakes toted cloth-covered trays to the Sanford Hotel and the room shared by the Texans. This was their first gesture of appreciation, and it was fortunate the trays were so heavy laden. Dan Fox was on hand. Sam Alper also. The hotelkeeper fetched extra chairs and, for a while, the atmosphere was almost festive, Blake relieved that his name had been cleared, Alper congratulating him on having acquired an astute lawyer, not to mention some uncommonly reliable helpers.

Larry, propped up by pillows, contentedly drinking coffee, became the focus of all eyes when Fox demanded his opinion.

"It's all over, huh? Or could young Daneman's killer still be runnin' free? C'mon, pal. You're the detective."

"If you have theories, I'd certainly like to hear them." declared the county attorney.

"All right, but just hunches — and a few hard facts," offered Larry. "Plain enough the widow found out I was plannin' a run to Polvadera. That spooked her. She wasn't countin' on some curious hombre learnin' about the other coat."

"Because of the implication." Alper nodded knowingly. "Clear proof somebody *had* impersonated Blake."

"Meanin' the killer," frowned Fox.

"Like Heisler told us, he'd do anything for her," Larry reminded him. "Plain enough she gave the order . . ."

"Passed sentence of death on you," said Irma, shaking her head sadly.

"And we thought she was the most beautiful . . ." began Jenny.

" . . . and Heisler set it up," continued Larry. "I got lucky and, from here on, we're talkin' of facts, not hunches. Wasn't only Heisler spooked when I showed up in court. The family lawyer, Forbes, knew him and Arlene were in big trouble, so he got out of there fast."

"He's the one you *weren't* leery of," said Stretch.

"And I should've been," Larry accused himself. "He was the right size and, bein' from the show business, Arlene could teach him how to walk like Andy, rig him in duds just like Andy's — and talk him into gettin' rid of young Jud. With Jud gone, she'd be next in line to collect the whole Daneman fortune."

"There's the motive," said Alper.

"Right," growled Fox. "Forbes was her man, but they kept it quiet. Wasn't nobody guessed."

"Thursby saw 'em make a run for it," said Larry. "Safe guess they had plenty to hide and — do we have to guess who put Andy's knife in Jud?"

"Forbes, it had to be Forbes," nodded Alper. "He and his paramour have paid the supreme penalty and nothing can save Heisler from a long term in prison. I'm told the other doctor saved his arm, but that's Heisler's only consolation now."

"One good thing about this whole dirty mess," remarked Fox. "Big Al's cousin in Oregon, him in the lumber business, won't want Box D nor the

Daneman herd."

"I suppose he'll look for a buyer," said Alper. "Well, he's next in line to inherit, so that's his privilege."

"I'm bettin' he'll collect all the cash, put the spread up for sale and head on back to Oregon," grinned Fox. "And it won't be the kinda spread it used to be. Mayor Stover and the council're gonna get back to running this territory."

"That's as it ought to be," opined Blake. "Not to speak ill of the dead, but Al Daneman had too much influence, and his hired hands took advantage of it," Having said that, he stroked his jaw, eyed the Texans curiously and asked, "Did you boys know Slow Wolf was such a — well — an educated man?"

"Slow Wolf!" Alper raised his eyes to the ceiling. "Ye gods! I'll never forget him, Judge Ewing certainly won't and I doubt anybody else will. He's one of a kind."

"We knew," grinned Stretch. "But

it's his secret, and he explained why."

"So much I owe him," reflected Blake.

"He don't see it that way," Larry assured him. "Saw it as his duty. Mighty strong on duty is our ol' buddy Slow Wolf."

Fox was the last guest to leave, and did not leave rightaway. He smoked a cigar and confided a hunch as to the outcome of the next elections in Platt County.

"Mayor Stover and his aldermen pals'll be reelected. You could make book Ray Thursby'll be our new sheriff. Warren Kepple won't nominate again and . . ."

"How about you, Dan?" asked Stretch.

"I don't need the responsibility nor the worries that come with it," shrugged Fox. "Thursby's welcome to Warren's star. Maybe he'll be a good sheriff, maybe he'll be a pain in the ass, but there's never no maybe about me. I'm content to be a deputy — and

I can take any sass Thursby hands out. Mert's wise to him too. We can handle him." He aimed a genial grin at Larry. "Smart move, me dealin' you in huh? You done good. I knew you'd sniff out the real killer. The only thing is. . . " He waxed apologetic, "I didn't count on you gettin' hurt."

Without bravado, Larry replied, "We're used to pain. It don't seem to matter to us no more."

"Ain't that the truth," Stretch sadly agreed. When Fox left them, he squatted on the edge of the other bed and matched stares with his partner. "So — uh — how long're we gonna hang around here?"

"Breakfast at Blake's manana," said Larry. "Then Henry'll be headed home to Polvadera in that real comfortable sprung rig, and he won't be travellin' lonesome."

"Sure," nodded Stretch. "You had to leave your cayuse in Polvadera. So, after that?"

266

"After that, just like always, we'll get to driftin' again," said Larry.

Stretch's rejoinder was familiar; he had said it many times.

"Well, we got nothin' better to do."

THE END

CALABOOSE EXPRESS
WHISKEY GULCH
THE ALIBI TRAIL
SIX GUILTY MEN
FORT DILLON
IN PURSUIT OF QUINCEY BUDD
HAMMER'S HORDE
TWO GENTLEMEN FROM TEXAS
HARRIGAN'S STAR
TURN THE KEY ON EMERSON
ROUGH ROUTE TO RODD COUNTY
SEVEN KILLERS EAST
DAKOTA DEATH-TRAP
GOLD, GUNS & THE GIRL
RUCKUS AT GILA WELLS
LEGEND OF COYOTE FORD
ONE HELL OF A SHOWDOWN
EMERSON'S HEX
SIX GUN WEDDING
THE GOLD MOVERS
WILD NIGHT IN WIDOW'S PEAK
THE TINHORN MURDER CASE
TERROR FOR SALE
HOSTAGE HUNTERS
WILD WIDOW OF WOLF CREEK
THE LAWMAN WORE BLACK

THE DUDE MUST DIE
WAIT FOR THE JUDGE
HOLD 'EM BACK!
WELLS FARGO DECOYS
WE RIDE FOR CIRCLE 6
THE CANNON MOUND GANG
5 BULLETS FOR JUDGE BLAKE
BEQUEST TO A TEXAN
THEY'LL HANG BILLY FOR SURE

FIGHTING RAMROD
Charles N. Heckelmann

Most men would have cut their losses, but Frazer counted the bullets in his guns and said he'd soak the range in blood before he'd give up another inch of what was his.

LONE GUN
Eric Allen

Smoke Blackbird had been away too long. The Lequires had seized the Blackbird farm, forcing the Indians and settlers off, and no one seemed willing to fight! He had to fight alone.

THE THIRD RIDER
Barry Cord

Mel Rawlins wasn't going to let anything stand in his way. His father was murdered, his two brothers gone. Now Mel rode for vengeance.

ARIZONA DRIFTERS
W. C. Tuttle

When drifting Dutton and Lonnie Steelman decide to become partners they find that they have a common enemy in the formidable Thurston brothers.

TOMBSTONE
Matt Braun

Wells Fargo paid Luke Starbuck to outgun the silver-thieving stagecoach gang at Tombstone. Before long Luke can see the only thing bearing fruit in this eldorado will be the gallows tree.

HIGH BORDER RIDERS
Lee Floren

Buckshot McKee and Tortilla Joe cut the trail of a border tough who was running Mexican beef into Texas. They stopped the smuggler in his tracks.

BRETT RANDALL, GAMBLER
E. B. Mann

Larry Day had the choice of running away from the law or of assuming a dead man's place. No matter what he decided he was bound to end up dead.

THE GUNSHARP
William R. Cox

The Eggerleys weren't very smart. They trained their sights on Will Carney and Arizona's biggest blood bath began.

THE DEPUTY OF SAN RIANO
Lawrence A. Keating and
Al. P. Nelson

When a man fell dead from his horse, Ed Grant was spotted riding away from the scene. The deputy sheriff rode out after him and came up against everything from gunfire to dynamite.

FARGO: MASSACRE RIVER
John Benteen

The ambushers up ahead had now blocked the road. Fargo's convoy was a jumble, a perfect target for the insurgents' weapons!

SUNDANCE: DEATH IN THE LAVA
John Benteen

The Modoc's captured the wagon train and its cargo of gold. But now the halfbreed they called Sundance was going after it . . .

HARSH RECKONING
Phil Ketchum

Five years of keeping himself alive in a brutal prison had made Brand tough and careless about who he gunned down . . .

FARGO: PANAMA GOLD
John Benteen

With foreign money behind him, Buckner was going to destroy the Panama Canal before it could be completed. Fargo's job was to stop Buckner.

FARGO: THE SHARPSHOOTERS
John Benteen

The Canfield clan, thirty strong were raising hell in Texas. Fargo was tough enough to hold his own against the whole clan.

PISTOL LAW
Paul Evan Lehman

Lance Jones came back to Mustang for just one thing — revenge! Revenge on the people who had him thrown in jail.

HELL RIDERS
Steve Mensing

Wade Walker's kid brother, Duane, was locked up in the Silver City jail facing a rope at dawn. Wade was a ruthless outlaw, but he was smart, and he had vowed to have his brother out of jail before morning!

DESERT OF THE DAMNED
Nelson Nye

The law was after him for the murder of a marshal — a murder he didn't commit. Breen was after him for revenge — and Breen wouldn't stop at anything . . . blackmail, a frameup . . . or murder.

DAY OF THE COMANCHEROS
Steven C. Lawrence

Their very name struck terror into men's hearts — the Comancheros, a savage army of cutthroats who swept across Texas, leaving behind a bloodstained trail of robbery and murder.

SUNDANCE: SILENT ENEMY
John Benteen

A lone crazed Cheyenne was on a personal war path. They needed to pit one man against one crazed Indian. That man was Sundance.

LASSITER
Jack Slade

Lassiter wasn't the kind of man to listen to reason. Cross him once and he'll hold a grudge for years to come — if he let you live that long.

LAST STAGE TO GOMORRAH
Barry Cord

Jeff Carter, tough ex-riverboat gambler, now had himself a horse ranch that kept him free from gunfights and card games. Until Sturvesant of Wells Fargo showed up.

McALLISTER ON THE COMANCHE CROSSING
Matt Chisholm

The Comanche, McAllister owes them a life — and the trail is soaked with the blood of the men who had tried to outrun them before.

QUICK-TRIGGER COUNTRY
Clem Colt

Turkey Red hooked up with Curly Bill Graham's outlaw crew. But wholesale murder was out of Turk's line, so when range war flared he bucked the whole border gang alone . . .

CAMPAIGNING
Jim Miller

Ambushed on the Santa Fe trail, Sean Callahan is saved by two Indian strangers. But there'll be more lead and arrows flying before the band join Kit Carson against the Comanches.

GUNSLINGER'S RANGE
Jackson Cole

Three escaped convicts are out for revenge. They won't rest until they put a bullet through the head of the dirty snake who locked them behind bars.

RUSTLER'S TRAIL
Lee Floren

Jim Carlin knew he would have to stand up and fight because he had staked his claim right in the middle of Big Ike Outland's best grass.

THE TRUTH ABOUT SNAKE RIDGE
Marshall Grover

The troubleshooters came to San Cristobal to help the needy. For Larry and Stretch the turmoil began with a brawl and then an ambush.